never too
CLOSE

www.chelleblis.com

CHELLE BLISS
USA TODAY BESTSELLING AUTHOR

CHAPTER 1
VITO

I PRESS print for what must be the hundredth time on my ma's ancient computer.

And nothing happens.

Again.

I hit the on/off button, check the power cables and connections, look for paper, ink, and any other obvious reasons why this goddamn little machine will print recipes and pictures of my mother's rescue animals, but the one day I actually need a physical document, I can't get the thing to show even the slightest sign of life.

"Come on, you little asshole."

I run my hands through my hair before I check the time on my phone.

Almost noon.

Damn it.

One of my mom's foster cats—this one is new, so I'm not sure what her name is—jumps up onto the desk and tries to nuzzle my face.

"Baby, you're adorable, but I don't have time for love right now."

I've showered, but I've still got to get dressed and drive down to the station. My meeting with the chief is in an hour, and I cannot fuck this up.

I scratch her before giving her a gentle nudge away from the desk, and then I check all the printer settings again. When another five attempts at printing still don't work, I give in and run up the stairs, and my sock snags on the wood. I catch myself before I fall flat on my face. "Oh fuck!" I yell out, aggravated beyond belief.

"Vito, language," my mother says, sitting at the dining room table with Sassy, one of her best friends.

Ma has a group of ladies she's tight with, and they keep one another busy. Sassy works as a waitress at my brother Benito's restaurant, Bev runs the local animal shelter where Ma volunteers, and then there is Carol, whose son and ex-husband own the garage here in Star Falls where my older brother Franco works.

Small-town living, but I wouldn't have it any other way.

I get my footing and stifle another mouthful of curses.

Sassy snorts and almost spits coffee onto Ma's tablecloth. "Mornin', sunshine," she says.

I go around the table and kiss Sassy and Carol on the cheeks, greeting them. "Bev workin'?" I ask.

When I get around to my mother, she gives me a fake-angry look but then holds up her hands to cup my face. "She'll be here for brunch in a few minutes. I'm so glad you're here, V. You can meet Sassy's niece."

I shake my head. "Can't stick around, Ma. Sorry. Got to run down to the station."

Ladies' brunch is a new thing they started after my sister Grace had her baby. Gracie is a stepmom to two adorable kiddos and has a one-year-old of her own now, Ethan. The brunches are potlucks where whoever is free can stop by and catch up. And Ma's friends are definitely birds of a feather. Even though only Sassy and Carol are here, at least ten dishes are on the table already.

"This spread could convince me to stick around," I say. "Sassy…" I draw out her name and flash her a flirtatious smile. "Are these your famous raspberry kolacky cookies?" I wink and grab one of the powdered-sugar-covered little bow ties.

"Vito," Ma sighs, swatting at my hand. "We have company coming today."

I shake my head. "Right, right, okay. Ma, can you help me for a sec? The damn printer's acting up again."

My mother crosses her arms over her chest, and the corner of one side of her lips curls up. "Aren't you the one who told me nobody uses paper anymore. Join the digital age?"

I shake my head and crack up at my mother's impersonation of me. "That doesn't sound like me, Ma. Sounds like you're confusing me with Benny."

Ma shakes her head but pushes back from the table. "Sassy, grab the door if anyone comes, will you? And if Eden arrives before I'm back, yell for me. This might take a minute."

I follow my mother down into the basement.

"Oh, kitty." Ma bends down to pet the cat who's still in isolation as soon as we make it to the bottom of the stairs. "How's my beautiful princess today?"

I squeeze my brows and try not to start stressing. "Ma," I say, trying to bring my mother back on task. "I just need these three pages printed. Can you take a look?"

I lean over the print preview panel, relieved that none of the text is readable. It's not that what I'm working on is a big secret or anything, but I just don't really want my family meddling in my business until I actually have news to share.

Ma immediately hits cancel on the print preview and drops into her office chair to get comfy. But then just as suddenly, she whirls to look at me. "Oh my God, son..."

"What? What is it?" My heart starts to race, and sweat instantly coats my palms. "Ma, what happened?" I rest a reassuring hand on her shoulder as my chest tightens.

Ma reaches a hand up to her shoulder and clenches my fingers between her perfectly manicured nails. "Baby," she says, looking sad. "Sassy just told me something upstairs. Something I don't know if you've heard about yet."

I squeeze her hand, all worries about the time evaporating because Sassy news isn't anything to panic over. "Ma, you're going to give me a heart attack. What is it?"

She stands from the chair and lifts her face to look from her five-foot-nothing frame into my eyes. "Vito, Michelle had dinner in your brother's restaurant last night. Michelle, son. She's moved back to Star Falls."

I'm so surprised by this that I drop Ma's hand and step away from her. "Michelle..." I mutter. "Wow. Well, okay. Is she all right? Her grandpa didn't get worse, did he?"

Michelle fucking Bianchi. My ex-wife. The woman who owned my heart and then literally crushed it under her stiletto heel.

Ma nods. "Looks that way. Sassy said her grandfather needs to move into a memory care place. You know that one on the east side of town."

I do know the one, but I don't say anything. I'm a firefighter, and there have been too many suspicious fires at that place over the last year. That's part of what I want to meet with the chief about. But I hold back what I know and focus on the fact that my ex-wife is back in town.

"I'm sorry to hear that. Michelle's gramps was a great guy," I add.

Ma nods. "But it looks like Michelle is doing very well for herself. She's opened her own business. Teaching at the community college too."

"Teaching?" I shake my head in wonder, but I'm not at all surprised. My ex-wife was always smart. Smart enough to leave my ass behind when it became clear we didn't have the same aspirations in life.

Aspirations. Even that word sounds smart. "I'm happy for her, Ma."

"Honey," Ma says, her caring eyes focused so intently on me I don't even have to guess what's coming. I know. My mother is so wonderful but also incredibly predictable. "Do you think you're going to be okay? Maybe you should see her? Sit down for a cup of coffee and just get everything out in the open."

I hold up my hands. "Nah, Ma. Michelle moving back to Star Falls is none of my business. We've been divorced for five years. I'm over it. I'm over her. All that's old news, ancient history, okay?"

Ma looks at me, an expression of so much worry and love on her face that I pull her in for a hug.

"What I really need right now is to get going, but I can't do that until I get this shit printed."

Her sadness seems to vanish instantly, but I know she won't be convinced so easily. "You got it, sweetie. I'm on it."

Thirty minutes later, I'm dressed in dark gray dress pants, a white shirt with the top few buttons unbuttoned, and I have a tie slung over my shoulder. I dig through my closet for some nicer shoes, but since Ma doesn't like us wearing shoes in the house, I loop my fingers through the laces to carry them to the door.

I look through my room for anything I can use to protect my paperwork and eventually have to settle on an old issue of one of my favorite camping magazines. I tuck the paperwork in, check the time, and haul ass down the stairs.

Just as I skid to a stop at the base of the stairs, my sister Grace raises an eyebrow at me and grins. "This little nugget has been asking for you for the last ten minutes."

"Gracie." I lean down to give my sister a kiss. "And look at you, little man. Got my hands full today, buddy. Hang on." I rush to the front door, drop my dress shoes, and gently set my magazine on top of them. Then I turn and open my arms wide to my nephew.

Gracie sets Ethan on his feet, and he struggles to make it all the way across the hallway. All thoughts about the time rush out of my head as I watch my nephew take shaky steps across the living room. His mouth is open in a thrilled grin, his arms in front of him as he reaches for me. I drop to my knees and inch across the floor just in time to catch him before his little legs buckle.

"What was that?" I ask, picking him up and

blowing loud kisses into his belly. "You run better than I do, buddy."

Little Ethan's baby teeth show as he laughs and laughs. He clamps his mouth against my shoulder and squeezes me tight in a hug.

"So proud of you, little man." I set my nephew down, and when I stand back up, he grabs my leg and tugs to be picked up again. "I got to run," I say reluctantly.

Ma's friends are gathered around the living room table, including Bev, who must have arrived while I was getting dressed.

"Bev." I blow her a kiss and wave. "Got to dash, ladies. Have a good brunch."

The smells of coffee and the sounds of happy chatter are so welcoming, for a minute, I consider texting my chief and canceling our meeting to stay home and hang out with my family and Ma's friends, who, after all these years, are family too. I look down at my nephew and catch a glimpse of the magazine that is protecting my list of accomplishments and my résumé.

I have a moment of self-doubt seize me so hard, I almost drop back onto my knees.

Ever since my divorce, I've been stuck. Lost.

Every time I get close to something that matters to me, I lose it, fuck it up, or run away.

I'm thirty-six, live at home with my parents, and haven't been on a real date in three months.

What I'm doing with my life, what I've done... I don't know.

I'm not like Benito, driven and intense in work and deeply committed to sowing my wild oats. My older brother Franco has had the same job for his whole life practically, and he has a woman he loves by his side. Gracie is an accomplished tattoo artist with two stepkids, a great husband, and now her own little nugget, Ethan.

I'm a middle child who's always been the lost kid. I thought that marrying Michelle was the answer to making the life I wanted, but turns out, I wasn't enough for her.

And I just got passed over for a promotion at work I wanted badly, but I wasn't enough for that either. For a hot second, I consider saying fuck it.

Dreams are for different people.

I could stay and eat brunch and hang with my family, but then what?

When everyone goes home to their lives, I'm going to go back upstairs to my bedroom and feel like shit about myself all over again?

I shake my head and smooth Ethan's hair. "Love you, kiddo, but I got to hustle up."

"Who you looking so sexy for, V?" Sassy gets up and heads over to pick up little Ethan. She lowers her voice. "Speaking of sexy, did your mother tell you who I saw last night?"

I stifle a groan.

The last thing I need is for my mom's friends to get into matchmaking mode.

Michelle is my past. She is most definitely not my future. She made that much clear when she divorced me.

"She did, Sassy, but you know that's old news. Nothing I'm going to get myself worked up over, and none of you need to either."

"What? What'd I miss?" Gracie pours some cream into her coffee and starts cutting up a child's plate full of food. "Who'd Sassy see?"

"Wish I could stay, but I'm late." I slip my feet into my shoes and tie the laces as fast as I can so Ma doesn't yell at me for running around without them tied. "Y'all can talk about me once I'm gone."

I check my pocket for my wallet and phone, then reach for the shelf Pops installed on the wall for my keys. But there's nothing hanging on the hook where my truck keys should be.

"Ma!" I yell. "Where are my keys?"

"Oh, shoot." Ma pushes back from the dining room table and pads over to me. I try not to think about the time. The chief is going to give me hell for this. "I'm sorry, honey. I moved your truck onto the street so the girls could park in the driveway. Your truck is down the street." She fishes the keys out of a pocket in her rhinestone-bedazzled jeans. "Here you go, baby. Have a great day, son."

I grab the keys, grin, and with the magazine in one hand, yank open the front door.

"Oh, uh…hello?" a soft voice says. Standing on the front stoop is probably the most stunning woman I've ever seen. And since my ex-wife was a stripper, that's saying something.

"Hello?" I look into her eyes and realize this woman is tall. Like nearly eye level with me, and I'm just shy of six feet. She's not skinny and lean like Michelle was. This woman is full-figured, which I cannot miss since she's holding a wriggling little girl about Ethan's age against her ample chest.

"Oh God. I'm so sorry. Did I knock on the wrong door?" The woman is staring at me, blinking her brown eyes rapidly. She squints and takes a step back, looking for the wrought-iron numbers that correspond to our street address on the front of the house.

"This is the Bianchi residence." I'm gripping the keys in my hand so tightly I feel the metal cut into my palm. I loosen my grip and cock my head. "Who are you looking for?"

"My aunt Shirley," she says, looking dazed. She frowns and pulls a cell phone from the front pocket of a large purse-style diaper bag. "I'm sorry to have bothered you."

She turns and starts to walk back down the walkway when I call out to her. "Shirley... Do you mean Sassy?"

Just then, Sassy bellows from the dining room table. "Eden!" My mom's friend bolts past me to meet the woman—Eden, I assume—at the door. "Oh my God," Sassy cries again. She takes the little girl from Eden's arms and plasters her face with kisses, then turns to me and holds out her arms. "Vito, hold my grandniece for a second. I need a hug from this one."

Before I know what's happening, there is yet another kid in my arms. "Uh, hello there," I say, holding the stranger's child awkwardly in my arms.

The little girl looks like she's about to start crying, and I don't blame her. I'm a strange man, and she was just yanked from her mama's arms. I plaster on a bright smile and sort of jiggle her up and down in my arms the way I do with Ethan. While I try to stall a meltdown, Sassy wraps Eden in her arms and rocks her wildly back and forth, tears literally streaming down her face.

"I'm so glad you're here now, baby. We're going to take good care of you."

With keys and my magazine in one hand and this kiddo in the other, I've literally got my arms full.

Sassy finally releases the woman whose cheeks are red even though she's wearing a smile so beautiful my heart cracks a little. She wipes tears from her eyes and leans her head on Sassy's shoulder, which takes some effort since Eden is tall.

"Vito, this is my niece, Eden. Newly landed in Star Falls from the City of Angels." Sassy hasn't released Eden for even a second, and I can't exactly extend a hand to shake hers, so I nod.

"Nice to meet you," I say, my words coming out slow as I look her over. I don't mean to be creepy, but this woman is a fucking knockout. But it hits me all at once that I'm holding her child. Her daughter. Which means a baby daddy or husband can't be far away. I steel my reactions to her and grin down at the little lady in my arms. "And who's this?" I ask.

Eden releases herself from her aunt's choke hold and wipes the last of her tears from her cheeks. "I'm sorry," she says. "You must think I'm a hot mess, just handing my baby to a stranger. This is my daughter, Juniper."

I drag my eyes away from Eden and grin at her child. "Juniper? What a gorgeous name for a gorgeous little lady. You know my nephew Ethan is about your age, and I'll bet you two are going to get along great." I raise my brows at Sassy, hoping she'll get the hint and take the kiddo so I can get going.

But Sassy is in no real rush to do anything but introduce Eden to absolutely everyone. She drags her niece into the living room, and I follow, keeping hold of Juniper while my mom, sister, Bev, and Carol all make their introductions to Eden.

"Ma," I say quietly, hoping I can appeal to her maternal instincts. As much as I hate to break up the party, if I'm late to meet the chief after we both agreed to come in on our day off, I can kiss this opportunity goodbye. "Ma, I've…"

But just as I'm walking up to my mother, hoping she'll take the baby from me, Juniper grabs everyone's attention by ripping out a belch so big that everyone in the room starts cracking up. Everyone but Eden.

"Oh no," she says, her arms out. She's moving toward me, her eyes fixed on her daughter as if she knows what's about to happen.

I'm still laughing in shock at the man-sized belch from the little kid when my shock turns to horror. Little Juniper looks up at me, her little lower lip trembles, and then she projectile vomits all over my dress clothes.

CHAPTER 2
EDEN

THIS IS NOT the reunion I'd imagined when my auntie invited me to her best friend's house. First of all, I was promised a ladies' brunch.

I know Auntie Shirley has a group of friends she's been tight with since high school. But nobody mentioned that any of those friends had hot sons. And the last thing I want anything to do with is a man. Any man. And especially a hot man.

Vito Bianchi is gorgeous. He had this heart-melting, youthful look about him when he was being playful with Juniper, but now, as he shrugs off the shirt that Juniper inconveniently threw up all over, it's like the gods of love and sex are tormenting me. He's got muscles for days. I can almost hear angels singing as he strips off the orange-splattered dress shirt.

17

I stare, stunned, while Lucia and my aunt grab Juniper and go wash her face in the kitchen. That leaves me with a whole bunch of people I don't know, including him.

"I'm so sorry," I blurt out. "She's not sick, I promise. She gets a little carsick sometimes, and I gave her some cold water with a tiny bit of orange juice in the car, but apparently that did not help."

Once the shock of what's happened wears off, I go immediately into damage-control mode. I rush toward the man and try to help him ease off the shirt so none of my daughter's throw-up touches his skin.

He shakes off the dress shirt and stands before me wearing just a sleeveless white tank and gray dress pants. My mouth opens a little at the sight of his sculpted chest dusted with a tiny hint of dark hair. His arms look so smooth, my fingers itch to touch the well-defined muscles.

"It's all right," he says, his voice sounding sincere. We're almost the same height, so when I lift my chin, our eyes meet. "I, uh... I'll just... I should change."

I'm holding the sticky shirt in my hands like it's yesterday's garbage while my traitorous eyes take in the length of him. "Your pants," I say, biting my lower lip.

He bends his head down to look, and he must see the big wet spot on the front of his pants, right over the zipper.

I want to die.

"I'm so sorry," I say again. "I'll have them cleaned. I'll replace them. I'm so sorry."

For a second, a look that is almost heartbreakingly sad passes over his face. He closes his eyes, then pulls his phone from his pocket. He's got a magazine and a set of keys in one hand, and with the other, he punches in a number on his phone.

"One sec," he tells me, then he turns his attention to the call. "Chief? Yeah, I'm going to be about fifteen minutes late. I got puked on. Thankfully by a child, but I've got to change."

He's quiet for a minute, then ends the call. He faces me with a smile that seems to spread across his whole face. "Could be worse. I could be the one who did the puking. At least I can still make my meeting."

"Oh God." The reality of what's going on hits me. He's dressed up. He was running out the door. And now, we've made him late. "What can I do? Do you have another shirt? Can I iron something?"

Vito looks at me for a second and laughs so hard, I am tempted to join in.

"Iron?" A woman who looks like a female version

of Vito is laughing with him. I just met her a minute ago, but I can't for the life of me remember her name. "My brother wears pajamas and house slippers twenty-four seven. He doesn't have another dress shirt."

Vito takes the dirty shirt from me and thrusts it at his sister. "Go stuff this in the laundry. Help your brother out."

She gives Vito a look but then holds out a hand. "Am I washing your pants too?"

For a hot minute, I hold my breath, wondering if he is actually going to strip off his pants right here in front of us all. But he just flicks his sister in the ribs and then takes the stairs two at a time.

While the hottie goes up to change, I head into the kitchen to see how my daughter is.

"Well, don't we make a fine first impression," I say, shaking my head. My aunt Shirley's meeting my daughter for the first time ever, but they seem to be getting along just brilliantly.

Juniper is sitting on the kitchen counter, her own shirt miraculously free of any signs of the mess. Her face is clean, and her hair has been smoothed back from her face. She's got a small bowl of water in front of her and one of those baby washcloths with a soft gray elephant attached to it. She's following my aunt's instructions and gently dabbing at her own cheeks with the cloth.

The sight breaks down a wall I have built around my heart, and I immediately burst into tears.

"Honey, it's okay." My aunt's friend Lucia is comedically short, so she comes over to comfort me but can't reach my shoulder. She rests a comforting hand on my lower back and just pats me. "Throw-ups happen. We have a lot of kids coming through this house. Believe me, we've seen worse."

My aunt has her hands firmly on Junie's waist, so she is secure, even sitting on the counter. "No more tears," my aunt insists. "We're family. Cleaning up messes comes with the territory."

But that's what Auntie Shirley doesn't understand. This is uncharted territory for me. I've had to hide Juniper for so long that having someone love her on sight is foreign to me. I just don't know how to accept this kind of love. This is why I left Los Angeles. I had no idea what I was getting myself into moving here. I had very few options left, though, and if this is how things are going to go, I can't imagine making a better decision.

Lucia wraps her arm around my waist. "You know, honey, how old is Juniper? One? She could be teething too. It might not just be carsickness. Those baby teeth are a real pain."

I wipe away the tears for the second time today and chuckle. "They are awful," I agree.

And she's right. Junie's been chewing and drooling so much lately, I'm sure that red spot I noticed on her gums the other day is another tooth about to break through.

"What do you say, Junebug?" I walk over to my aunt and rest a hand on Shirley's shoulder. I don't want to pull my daughter from her great-aunt before they have a chance to bond. Junie's only had me as a caregiver for most of her life. I'm thrilled she seems so interested in all the new people that she's not clinging to me.

"Mama, elephant." Junie dunks the washcloth into the water, sending a small sprinkle of water onto my aunt's sleeve.

"I see it," I say, grinning at my baby.

"Juniper is gorgeous," Lucia says. "What an angel. You know who's going to love her? My grand-daughter. She loves her cousin Ethan, but..." Lucia waves a hand at my daughter's curls. "Look at that hair. She's going to want to play princess and dress-up. I hope you're ready for playdates and lots of willing babysitters."

I cover my mouth with my hand to hold back any words that might come out. There's nothing I can say to this. I can finally see why my aunt was so insistent on my moving here. After everything that happened back in Los Angeles, I believe that I can start over here in Star Falls. When I first found out I was pregnant, I thought my big, exciting life was over. And then, when Juniper's father made his feelings about the matter clear to me, I thought my life itself was over.

My aunt lifts Junie off the counter while I take the bowl of water and dump the contents down the drain. I'm facing the sink and window when a sexy voice calls into the kitchen.

"Ma, I'm going for real now. See you for dinner."

I turn to follow the voice and see Vito Bianchi standing in the doorway. The waves of his brown hair have fallen loose from their careful style, and in place of the perfect dress shirt and pants, he's wearing a pair of dark jeans and a casual cotton button-down.

"Do you really only have one dress shirt?" I blurt out. As soon as I say the words, I shake my head. No freaking filter. I never have had one. "I mean, you look great. I was serious about replacing your shirt and pants. If, you know…" I'm rambling.

Lucia raises up on her tiptoes to kiss her son's

cheek, but over his mother's shoulder, his eyes are laser-focused on me. "See you, V," she says. But then Lucia cocks her head as if putting something together in her mind. "Are you going to work? I didn't think you were on today?"

Vito's intense chocolate eyes move from mine to his mom. "Ma, it's something else. I'm meeting with the chief, but it shouldn't take long. See you for dinner."

"Vito, are you in trouble? Honey, is everything all right?" She sounds worried, and right away, I pick up on the smallest details in Vito's reaction.

He visibly winces and kind of pulls away, but then he quickly composes himself and reassures his mom. "Ma, it's nothing." Then he breaks into a grin and lowers his chin to look at Junie. "Bye, Juniper. You sure know how to make an entrance." Then it's my turn. "Nice meeting you, Eden." His voice is softer when he addresses me.

I don't have the energy to apologize again. I'm starting to feel overwhelmed by the emotions of the day, and I've only been here for like twenty minutes.

I nod at him. "Nice meeting you," I say quietly, then I turn away.

Hot guy or not, I can only let so many things get close to my heart right now. Bringing an aunt and a bunch of new friends in is more than enough and maybe even more than I can take.

———

By the end of brunch, I've laughed so hard and eaten so much, my stomach is turning. My aunt has convinced me to call her Aunt Sassy, because she said every time I say Shirley, no one knows who I'm talking about.

And honestly, the Aunt Shirley I expected is nothing like the aunt I'm seeing. Sassy fits her so, so much better.

It has to be around one thirty when Gracie puts her son down for a nap in her old bedroom upstairs. She yawns and asks her mom to wake her by 2:30 if she isn't up so she can get on the road to pick up her older kids.

Bev hurries back to the shelter, and Carol has a job she's got to get back to as well. Lucia doesn't have a full-time job, and Aunt Sassy doesn't have to be at work where she's a waitress until three. After Grace lies down with Ethan, Lucia and Aunt Sassy put away the leftover food but then retreat to the couches.

"Are you allergic to dogs?" Lucia asks.

"Not at all. I love dogs," I tell her. "I've actually been planning on getting one now that we have a little house."

"Oh, Eden, don't tell Lucia you want a dog. She'll have every rescue from that shelter on your doorstep if you let her." Aunt Sassy leans back on the couch, crosses her legs, and plops her bare feet up on a pretty ottoman.

"Well, my Chihuahua isn't friendly," Lucia warns. "But she loves Gracie. I'm going to send her upstairs. But my Venus is the sweetest. She's been out in the yard plenty for one day." Lucia opens a patio door, and an aged lab-mix-type dog wanders in, wagging her tail so hard it's difficult not to grin. After loving on the lab for a few minutes, Lucia scoops up the Chihuahua and carries it upstairs. "Be right back, girls."

Once my aunt and I are alone, I get down on the floor with Junie and introduce her to the dog. "See, Junie?" I hold my hand out, fingers down, letting the dog sniff me. "Hold Mommy's hand."

I clasp Junie's hand in mine and let the dog sniff her fill. Once she seems satisfied that we're good people, she licks Junie's hand and flops down on her back, legs up.

"I think that means we can pet her," I say,

scratching the silvery fur with my nails.

"Venus is an angel," Aunt Sassy says over a yawn. "I never worry about the kids around that one. The Chihuahua, on the other hand…"

Lucia returns and drops onto the couch next to Sassy. "You girls want some more coffee or water?"

"Lucia, I'm stuffed. I'm not going to be able to make it through my shift without a bottle of Tums."

I look at my aunt. "Auntie, are you okay?"

Aunt Sassy pats her belly. "Baby, never better. Don't you worry about me. But just you wait. You hit fifty, and nothing works the same anymore."

Lucia cackles her agreement. "What I wouldn't give to be fifty again," Lucia says. "I'm just grateful I have grandchildren while I'm still young enough to enjoy them."

"Amen." Sassy yawns again. "Lucia, I don't know where you get the energy. One afternoon with the kids has worn me out." She looks at me. "And you. You've been doing this all alone."

An awkward silence fills the room. I don't know what to say to that. I assume my aunt's told her friends about our family. My aunt is my dad's sister, but calling the man my dad would be… Well, let's just say calling him that would be generous.

He left my mom when I was three and didn't

bother to parent beyond sending child support—late, and usually less than what he owed—and cards on my birthday and holidays.

If Aunt Shirley hadn't made an effort to stay in touch with me my entire life, I wouldn't know anyone on my dad's side of the family.

And then there's my mom. That's a whole different kind of story, and it's even sadder than being abandoned by my dad.

"How you doing, honey?" Lucia asks warmly. And somehow, even though I've only just met her, I get the sense that she really does care.

"What I want to know," Sassy interrupts, not letting me answer Lucia's question, "is what's up with Juniper's father? What is it with these men who abandon their kids?" Sassy shakes her head and looks at Lucia. "You know I don't condone the kind of father my brother was. But it really pisses me off that my beautiful niece had to go through this not just with her own father, but with the father of this beautiful angel."

Lucia and Sassy look incredibly worked up, and while I appreciate their interest, this is not a conversation I'm comfortable having. No, correction. It's not a conversation I can have. There's a whole legal contract that prevents me from saying just about anything more than the rehearsed line I'm about to repeat.

"We reached an amicable agreement," I say quietly. "I want to raise my daughter on my own. I didn't want to raise her in Los Angeles. It's better for all of us this way."

The answer is close to the truth of the situation. Close enough, but I still get a very sad look from Lucia and a shade of stink-eye from Aunt Sassy.

My aunt frowns. "Well, that asshole doesn't know what he's missing out on."

"Ma, seriously. You going to ground Sassy for that kind of language?"

I look up from my perch on the floor to see Vito leaning against the living room doorway.

And sweet Jesus…somehow, he looks even better than he did earlier.

"V, baby, I didn't even hear you come in. You hungry? We got loads of leftovers. Let me make you a plate." Lucia jumps up before he can accept. She passes by him, and he gives her a kiss as she heads to the kitchen.

Then he strolls past me and takes Lucia's seat next to my aunt on the couch. "You know she wouldn't listen if I told her no," he says, grinning at my aunt. "So, who's the asshole?"

Sassy shakes her head and frowns. "Nobody that matters, that's for sure."

"Fair enough," Vito says. He kicks up his feet and shares the ottoman with my aunt. The gesture is so comfortable, so familiar. I can't believe this is the life my aunt's lived all these years. A pang of longing hits me deep in my chest, and I do what I always do now when the hard feelings close in. I shake them off.

I crawl over to Junie's diaper bag and pull out her favorite toy, a little fabric book with large felt pieces that can be stuck to the pages of the book. I focus on my daughter but address my question to Vito.

"So, uh, how was your meeting?" I settle Junie in my lap and cross my legs to form a chair for her little body. She tears the fabric teddy bear and carrots and cars off the book and then sticks them back on in different places. I avoid making eye contact as I ask the question, but I peek up at him as he answers.

"Good, I guess." He's quiet, his full lips pressed together. He studies my face, and for a moment, I feel like he's going to say more, but then he just says, "Thanks for asking."

I fix my attention on Junie while Lucia comes back in with a plate of food for Vito. "Oh honey, I didn't grab you anything to drink. What do you want?"

Vito takes the plate from his mom and motions to the couch. "Ma, sit. I'll get myself a water. Take a load off, will you? You've been running all day. Hang with your friends."

He takes his plate and wanders off toward the kitchen. I can't even help myself. As he passes by, I check out his ass.

And man, that was the wrong thing to do. It's a really, really nice ass.

I drag my eyes away just as Sassy and Lucia settle in for their next pointed question.

"So, Eden," Lucia asks. She rubs her hands together gleefully while Sassy rolls her eyes and groans. "What kind of dog are you thinking?"

I chuckle and kiss the top of my daughter's head.

Welcome to Star Falls.

I have a feeling I'm going to like living in a small town a lot more than I ever dreamed was possible.

CHAPTER 3
VITO

THE ONE BAD thing about living in a small town is sometimes you have to go far outside your comfort zone.

One thing that was never in my comfort zone was school—specifically, college. But ever since our meeting last week, the words of my chief keep echoing in my ears.

I'm a firefighter. Been a firefighter since I was twenty. I toyed around with a bunch of jobs—some I liked and a few I even liked a lot. And I admit there were a few I got fired from, but shit, I was a kid back then.

What I always knew was that I was not cut out for college. Nobody in my family went to college. Gracie is a self-taught artist who started tattooing right out of high school. Franco's a mechanic. Benito did go to culinary school, but that's a totally different type of learning. I mean, there's no math required in culinary school—at least not as far as my brother said. Kitchen math, sure, like measuring, budgets, and shit. But the kind of stuff that put me to sleep in high school? Algebra and whatnot... I just couldn't see spending four years and a load of money to learn stuff I'd never use in my life.

When I met with the chief, I asked him point-blank about my future. Fourteen years with the department. Excellent reviews and commendations. But I'm the only one who hasn't been promoted. Last month, I applied for two jobs—captain in a city department about an hour away from Star Falls and inspector here in town.

I didn't get either.

I didn't even get an interview.

I had the blessing of the chief to apply for the inspector position, but until the final decision was made, I couldn't really ask him about what I need to do to move up.

When we finally sat down, the answer should have been obvious, but I was still surprised when I heard it.

"There's no question you're a good guy and a

great firefighter." Chief shoved the reading glasses off his face and dropped my résumé and list of career accomplishments on his desk. "You know how in-demand these jobs are. Every firefighter in the state would love to move to a place like Star Falls for a six-figure job working investigations. Every time we post an opening, we get more candidates than we can possibly imagine." Chief pointed at me with a single finger. "How many you think applied for the job you wanted? Throw out a number."

I shook my head and sighed. "I don't know, a hundred."

Chief blew air out from between his lips. "V, we had almost two thousand applications come in. Two thousand. We had guys applying from as far as New York and Alaska."

"Two thousand applicants..." I repeated in disbelief.

I knew that the hiring process was often political and came down to who you knew and who knew you, but shit, with that many people, I can understand why I wasn't even interviewed. I couldn't compete with that many guys. A job I'd thought I'd be perfect for, but I was never, ever close to being considered, let alone close to getting it.

"Vito, some of those guys had PhDs. P-h-fucking-

Ds." He raised his silver brows and sighed. "Incredible on paper, great references. At this level, the quality of the careers is next level." He met my eyes and shrugged. "It's like anything else. I don't think a piece of paper from a college makes a bit of difference to whether or not I want you in my company. But it's a box the powers that be can check, and it makes the process a lot simpler."

A box they can check.

Four years of somebody's life, maybe more, for the education, not to mention the money, the cost. And for what? After taking some classes on dead poets and basic math, some dickhead with a degree is a more attractive candidate than me after fourteen years on the job?

Even as my gut burned with frustration, I knew Chief was giving it to me straight. There are no undereducated firefighters getting inspector and captain positions. It's the guys who have the time in I do *and* the piece of damn paper to back it up who are edging me out time and time again.

The meeting we had was all the confirmation I needed. I had no path forward in my career.

I'm thirty-four years old, and the one thing holding me back from moving ahead in my career is a damn college degree.

But that's the reason I've spent some of my time on my days off trolling the internet, reading up on local colleges. When I look at the courses that are offered, the application process, the requirements to get in, and then the courses I'd have to take, it sends me off into a funk that has me questioning everything.

I slam the lid of my laptop down a little too hard and check the time. It's almost sunrise, and I've got two hours until my next shift starts.

I tug on a T-shirt and slide into my house shoes before quietly heading down the stairs since Ma and Pops are still asleep.

When Gracie lived here, she didn't start work until after noon, and I had early mornings completely to myself. Now that Pops is retired, he's eased off his sleep schedule. Most of the days I'm on shift, I have coffee with Pops before I head out. It's an oddly comforting routine.

I try not to spend a lot of time thinking about it, but the reality is that every time I get in my truck and go to work, it could be the last time I see my family.

Star Falls is a small town, but there are enough smells and bells to keep our department hopping. Smells being anything from someone thinking they smell gas to smelling actual smoke, and bells meaning everything you could imagine. Falls at nursing homes, home alarms, smoke detectors going off because somebody thought cooking a pizza in a toaster was a thing.

And of course, we see our share of horrific stuff. Accidents. Injuries. Fatalities. Homes destroyed. Precious possessions lost.

Most people spend their lives running from danger and scary shit. When you're a first responder, I don't care what kind, the only way to do the job is to get up close with the stuff that gives other people nightmares.

Staring into the soot that covers the windows of a burning business. Crawling along the floor of a hallway thick with smoke. I've carried kids out of car wrecks with broken bones and injuries that haunted me for months. Wiped the debris off the face of an old lady who couldn't escape her apartment before the floor of her kitchen collapsed beneath her walker. I've smelled things and seen things most people will live their whole lives and never even think about.

After Michelle divorced me, I moved back home. I was heartbroken and never considered living on my own. I don't know why. A lot of guys lose their wives and relationships because of the stresses of the job, but for me, I need the routine of my family. The fact that no matter what I've seen during the shift, no matter how ugly and awful, the world I love and trust keeps spinning.

When I was married to Michelle, I desperately needed that innocence. I needed to know that I could come home to my wife, and she'd be there wanting me to watch some dumb-ass show while we argued over whether to get pepperoni on the whole pizza or only half.

I needed a strong family to anchor me to something that felt stable and real. When that ended, I went back home and never considered living anywhere else. Living under my parents' roof may be a massive strain on my dating life, but I don't think I could keep doing this work without some normal, non-fire-related life to go back to.

There are guys in my company who come from generations of firefighters. Guys whose dads and grandfathers and, in some cases, wives and mothers made careers in the fire service. I think they get a lot out of having people who understand the unpre-dictable schedule, the wrecked sleep, the hours, and the physical toll of the work.

But not me.

When I leave work, I switch off as much as I can. I'm never not a firefighter, but it's sometimes nice just to be Vito Bianchi, middle child, lost in the noise of my life outside of work.

When I head downstairs, I'm a little disappointed that Pops isn't up. Sometimes he surprises me by sneaking down when I'm in the shower or even before I'm awake. But nobody is sipping coffee or reading the paper at the table. I smell the coffee that I brewed before I jumped in the shower, and I pet the dogs who are so old now, they don't do much more than give me a one-eyed glare before going back to sleep.

I fill a mug and stare into the darkness outside the kitchen window. I can't help but think of Michelle being back in town.

Fuck, it's been a long time since I saw her. A long time since I had sex with anyone. And even longer since I was in a relationship with anyone who I thought could live up to what I had with my ex-wife.

My mom's words come back to me, and I wonder if it would do any good to see her again.

I finish my coffee and get ready to head to the station. I'm not sure why today, of all days, I'm wishing my pops were there to nod at me over his reading glasses, but I feel like I'm literally heading into the fire today.

And I'm not sure I like the feeling.

The call for a structure fire comes in close to midnight. The address is a residence in a neighborhood a short distance from the firehouse, which is good news because we know from dispatch there's a baby on the scene.

We scramble to get into gear and load into the engine, with the lights going but no siren. It's standard operating procedure if we don't need to clear traffic to run without sirens after bedtime.

When we reach the location, a woman is standing in the street in front of her house. She's wrapped in a knee-length bathrobe and is barefoot, cradling a screaming baby against her chest. The minute the crew leaves the engine, the chief greets the homeowner and assesses what he can. Within seconds, he's calling out orders.

The scene is surprisingly calm, all things considered. The company falls into our rhythm, uncoiling the hose and wrenching the nearby hydrant. Chief calls out that the homeowner is unsure of the origin, reported smoke in the bathroom, and the bathroom fan was on maybe thirty minutes.

Chief's calling out that there's no husband, just the woman and baby, who appear upset but unharmed. Everyone's out. That's a good start. Even with no reported people or pets inside, we'll still have to check every room just to make sure.

There have been a few people who've locked an unwanted spouse in a closet and tossed in a match, so we can't just take the homeowner's word for it when they say the place is empty. Chief sends two vets, Miller and Drinan, on a single attack line while we wait for reinforcements to arrive.

Chief is standing at the back of the ambulance where the homeowner and her baby have been checked out for any signs of exposure to smoke or fumes. They're wrapped in blankets against the chilly night made even colder by the fact that they were both barefoot from the quick look I got when we pulled up.

The fire was contained to the bathroom and the hallway, and it looked like the fan was most likely the cause. The bathroom fan had a buildup of dust and dirt. Not uncommon at all, but most people don't realize that the fans should be cleaned.

I feel bad for the woman. Looks like they hadn't moved in all that long ago. Moving boxes were still stacked in the corners of each room. But the house is so small, very few of her possessions will be salvageable between the smoke and the water.

Only once the cleanup is nearly complete and the chief asks me to escort the homeowner inside do I realize I know the lady. And I know her baby.

"Eden?" I've got all my turnout gear in place, so I'm not even sure she can see my face. "It's Vito. Vito Bianchi."

Since I'm on the job, I keep my demeanor professional, but inside, my heart is breaking for her. She just moved to town. She's not even unpacked yet. And now she's lost everything. She's literally wearing a blanket.

Eden's face drops when I say my name. Her lovely face is pale, and she looks like she's both exhausted and in shock. I'm sure she is both. Even worse, little Juniper is quiet, sound asleep against her mom's neck. Eden doesn't look like she wants to move or walk, let alone go into her house.

"Hey," I say, nodding. "I can take you inside. Let's get your purse, your cell phone. You're going to need to stay someplace. Can we call Sassy?"

Eden's eyes are unblinking, staring at me. She shakes her head slowly.

I take a few steps away from Eden and ask what time it is. The captain calls back that it's four in the morning. My shift ends in a couple of hours, but she's not going to be able to sit out here shivering in a blanket until then.

"Eden," I repeat, putting a gloved hand on her shoulder. Through the blanket, I can feel her trembling. "Listen. I'm going to help you. Let's get your purse and your phone. Let's take this one step at a time."

She's staring at the house, soft purple shadows under her brown eyes. "What happened?" she asks. "I didn't…I didn't leave any candles burning."

"I know," I assure her. "This was not your fault at all. We think the bathroom fan overheated. Come on. Let's go inside and get what we can."

This part is going to be hard. Most people don't realize that even a small fire could destroy the contents of the house.

I know from the attack crew that the bathroom had burned, and I mean burned. The flames had been contained to one room, but the smoke, soot, and ash got everywhere. I just hope we can find credit cards, keys, her identification. Hopefully, a pair of shoes that can be salvaged if she's lucky.

The excitement and adrenaline of the night start wearing off, and I stifle a yawn. I haven't slept at all this shift, so pretty soon, I'll have been awake for a full twenty-four. Not ideal, but there are shifts where I can't catch any rest between calls. Then there are some shifts where the most excitement is whether the chief's going to bitch because someone put too much pepper in the chili.

"You ready?" I let my hand fall to where I think the small of Eden's back is beneath the thick protective blanket she's got wrapped around her like a sheet.

"Is it safe?" She suddenly comes to life and shakes her head. "Wait, Vito..." She looks down at Juniper and shakes her head again. "I don't want to take her in there. The smoke, there could be toxins..."

I can't say I blame her. The fire is out, and the smoke has cleared, but with the stench of ash and the particles in the air, I wouldn't let my baby go inside that place either.

She looks down at her bare toes and lets one side of the blanket fall open. "Will you take her?" she asks, her eyes wide and her voice unsteady. "I'll be quick. My purse should be on the counter in the kitchen. I think my phone was on the charger in the kitchen too. I won't be long."

The kitchen is at the front of the little house, and the bathroom is all the way at the back. Not that that means a whole hell of a lot now, but at least she won't have to try to sift through the point of origin.

I reach out my arms, and Eden manages to slip

Juniper into my hold without jostling her too much. She sets her in my arms like a baby, not upright against my shoulder like she was sleeping on her mom, which is good because I would rather not have her face against my filthy turnout gear.

Eden tucks the blanket tightly around her daughter, then meets my eyes. "Thank you," she says, then starts to walk away from me toward the wide-open front door.

The captain sees her leaving my side and, taking note of the kid in my arms, nods at me and follows after her to make sure she gets in and out quickly.

"Property owner's been notified." Chief stands beside me and watches as Eden tiptoes past the dark entryway of the house.

"Owner?" I echo. "This place is a rental?"

Chief nods. "Tenant moved in just a couple days ago, sounds like. I told the property owner they didn't need to come out, but Bob Horton owns this place. He panicked and said he's on his way."

"Horton owns this place? The electronics guy? Since when does he own rental property?" As I talk with Chief, I can't help but watch Juniper sleep. She looks so peaceful and so, so beautiful. Like her mom.

Chief laughs, but he softens his voice a bit when the baby squirms. "Yeah, Horton is apparently branching out. I told him he'd need to take a closer look at his cleaning and maintenance protocol before he rents a place again."

I shake my head. "How long did Bob own this place before he rented it? Five minutes?" A low burn of anger builds in my chest. "This is the shit that lights me up," I say, trying hard not to pace in place and wake Juniper. "Bob bought this house, probably on the cheap, did nothing to fix it up, and rented to a single mother with a baby. Horton have insurance? She's going to lose everything."

He nods. "She has renters, and he has insurance on the place. It'll take some time, but she'll be all right."

Little Juniper shivers as though she's having a terrible nightmare.

I rock her lightly in my arms and watch as the captain follows Eden back through the front door. She is wearing a pair of sneakers and the knee-length robe. She has the same diaper bag I saw at my parents' slung over her arm, and she looks far from all right.

I make a vow to myself there and then to make it my business to see that she and Juniper come through this better than just okay.

CHAPTER 4
EDEN

WHEN THEY SAY you don't know what you've got till it's gone… Well, I'm living that now.

I know everything I lost in that damn house fire. My clothes, my kid's clothes. Junie's toys, my books. Talk about taking stock of your life. No matter how much stuff I lost, none of that mattered.

Not as long as I have my baby and myself.

We can make it through anything.

Within a few days of the fire, the house was officially taken over by the insurance company, and I had to make an inventory and say goodbye to everything I'd just paid to move across the country.

But the simple fact is, every day I wake up thankful that Junie and I were awake when it started. Thankful that I had renters insurance. Thankful that I had a caring local agent who stood by me when the company grilled me about the claim. That was no fun.

I gave recorded statements about how long I left the bathroom fan on. What I did, where I was, what I was wearing. Even what I had to drink. As if I'd get so plastered as a single mom that I'd burn down a house with my kid in it.

It all happened so fast.

I was going to take a shower before bed, so I turned on the bathroom light and the exhaust fan so the steam wouldn't fog up the bathroom. Just before I was about to step into the shower, I decided to take a bath instead. I left the bathroom to get a book, heard Junie calling for me from her crib, and I went in and checked on her. I changed her wet diaper, but before I could put her back to sleep, I smelled smoke.

And then, the scariest few hours of my life happened. I thought I'd been through some rough stuff up until then. And while I'm not proud of how I got the money, I have the means to replace what we lost. We have insurance. I have a little nest egg. And pretty darn soon, Junie and I might actually have our own house.

The extended-stay hotel the insurance company put us up in is comfortable, and Aunt Sassy has visited us every day—in fact, she's pestered me to stay with her while we get through this whole mess. But my aunt has a small one-bedroom unit.

She's in her sixties and still working on her feet as a waitress. She has a great life, but she's done a lot already, and just welcoming me and Juniper into her life is generous enough.

Junie is playing on a brand-new playmat on the floor of the bedroom we've been sharing in the hotel while I flip between images of houses on my phone and the local community college catalogue.

Ever since the fire, Vito Bianchi has been texting me every day he's not working to check in on me and Juniper. It's sweet and very chill.

I never get the sense that he's flirting, not that I'd mind if he did. I never really thanked him for being so kind to me the night of the fire. It was all such a shock. I didn't realize he was a firefighter, so I had the hardest time in the moment recognizing who he was.

But since that night, I have to be honest, I think about handsome Vito Bianchi—and I think about him a lot. Too much.

And ever since I moved to Star Falls, I've been thinking about what comes next. I have ten years of guaranteed income and some money set aside for

Junie's education, but the reality is, time is going to pass, and I'm going to need a career.

I can't imagine spending ten years out of the workforce to raise my daughter as a single mom is going to make for a really impressive future résumé.

"What should we do today, Junebug?" While my daughter chews on a plastic spatula, I hold up one finger on my right hand. "Junie," I say, trying to get her to follow the numbers. "One means we go to college and check out the campus." Then I hold up two fingers on my left hand. "And two means we go shopping for a new house."

I smile at her and hold up both hands. "One or two, Junie? One or two?" I hold up the corresponding fingers to help reinforce the numbers while I let my sweet girl pick our plan for the day.

Junie climbs up onto her bare feet and reaches one hand toward my right hand and the other toward my left. "One, two," she laughs.

I pick her up and cuddle her close. She smells sweet and fresh, her soft brown curls silky against my cheeks. I smooch her and blow ticklish raspberries against her neck.

"You want it all, huh? One and two."

She laughs hard and kicks her feet, so I put her down and she drops to the playmat to grab a toy.

I check the time. It's only half past nine in the morning. We have no insurance calls to make, no clothes or furniture to replace. We have the whole day ahead of us, and I am hell-bent on making my future in Star Falls a lot better than the first couple of weeks have been.

"So, it's settled," I say. "Let's do both."

I call a local real estate agent and inquire about a few properties. Once I get through to someone and share the properties I saw online, a nice woman named Taylor agrees to call me back as soon as she can set up viewings.

"I might not be able to set them all up today," she warns. "But I believe at least two of the properties have lockboxes, so with some notice, we should be able to get inside."

Taylor takes some information from me, including my name, current address, and my driver's license number. I'm a little hesitant to give that out over the phone, but then she explains it's a safety precaution they put in place for the agent's sake.

"We'd like you to take a picture of your license and text that to this number," she tells me. "Along with the names and ages of all the people who will be attending the walk-through."

"Oh," I say. "Okay. How soon do I need to get you that information?"

"An hour before the first showing, I'll check the system and make sure we have everything we need. So, the sooner you can get that over, the better. But at the latest, one hour before we actually plan to meet. Of course, we don't have firm plans now, so if you can get things to me this morning, we should be good to go as soon as I have time slots confirmed."

"I can do that," I tell her. "The only thing I'm not sure about is the age of one of the people in my party." A slow smile spreads over my face. "I mean, I need to confirm that he's even available. I am new to town, and I only have a few local friends."

"How sweet, Eden. Where did you move here from?"

I give her the standard song and dance. Moved from LA, single mama, one-year-old baby.

She asks me the usual questions—did I ever see anyone famous, is LA traffic as bad as they say, do I miss the weather?

I did, in fact, see many famous people—it was part of my job. But since those so-called celebrities were also my undoing, I give my standard answer to that question too. "I once sat in a booth at a diner behind Keanu Reeves."

That's actually true. I did, so I don't have to embellish too much for that story.

After I answer all Taylor's questions—yes, in person, he looks exactly like he does in movies, and no, I didn't speak to him. Yes, he seemed really, really nice. I confirm that yes, LA traffic is the worst, and yes, I do miss the weather a little.

"But I really love the seasons," I explain. "I'm enjoying having a real fall here in the Midwest."

After we've exhausted her questions, she reminds me to send over my license and the names, and she promises to send over a time as soon as she's set up some showings.

Before I send over my driver's license, I grab my phone and hover a finger over the text messages. I pull up one hunky firefighter's number, and before I can talk myself out of it, I send off a text.

Me: Weird question. Two, actually. How old are you, and are you off work today by any chance?

My heart thumps against my ribs, and I start grinning like an idiot. Is he going to think I'm too forward?

As the minutes pass by and I don't get any answers, I start to spiral into embarrassment.

I'm an idiot. I should text him back and say never mind. Just then, my phone chirps with a text alert.

Vito: I'm thirty-four, and I'm free as a bird. Off until Sunday. Whatcha got?

My palm starts sweating, and my cheeks heat.

Me: I don't want to lure you in under false pretenses, but could I hire you as an informal fire safety inspector? Payment is lunch at the restaurant of your choice as long as it's kid-friendly.

He responds this time in seconds.

Vito: You said my two favorite words. Fire and food. But I am curious why you need my age. I'm not going to pass for under twelve if you're going for a kid's meal discount.

I shake my head and stifle a small giggle while a little tiny spark of excitement blooms in my chest.

Me: I must disclose the names and ages of anyone I want to take on a house showing today. I called a real estate agent. Hence the need for someone who might help me not rent another deathtrap of a house. Maybe this time, I'll buy, but I'd love a hand inspecting things that I never knew existed. Like fan vents...

He sends back a crying laughing emoji and a thumbs-up emoji.

Vito: Let me know where and when. But do me one favor?

I send back just a simple question mark.

Vito: Maybe don't give Juniper OJ in the car…

I full-body laugh at that and send back a long line of cracking up and mind-blown emojis. Then I drop the phone and take a picture of the front and back of my newly minted Ohio license and text it to Taylor along with our names: Eden Byrne, 26, Juniper Byrne, 14 months, and Vito Bianchi, 34.

Seeing our names together like that makes us look like a little family. I shut down the thoughts before they can even take hold.

"No boys, Junebug." I drop down onto the playmat and pretend to cook up an over-easy plastic egg on a little blue skillet. "No boys, no dating. Just friends."

She mouths something that sounds like, "Nahlalaha mends," and I give her a high five.

I can't pretend, though, that I'm not looking forward to meeting my hot new friend later today. Sigh. Maybe my closed-down heart isn't as shut off as I'd thought.

Let's just hope, this time, I don't get burned.

―――――――

Vito arrives at the hotel where I'm staying a full thirty minutes earlier than I'd asked. He asked if we could go over some stuff before we look at any houses, and I agreed.

When I open the door of my hotel room, he's looking freshly showered and hotter than I remember. He's wearing blue jeans, bright-blue running shoes, and a tight black T-shirt. It's a gorgeous fall day, but both Junie and I are dressed in layers in case it gets too warm or too cool. Vito's got his arms out to hug me, and with his hair slicked back, sunglasses over his eyes, and a sexy grin on his face, it takes everything inside me to stop myself from knocking him over and wrapping my legs around his waist.

He's just a friend, I remind myself.

I lean in for a chaste hug, pat him on the back, and then hurriedly pull away before his cologne or his soap or whatever fucking erotic scent I sniffed in that two-second hug becomes my undoing.

Damn my libido. She's a clueless bitch. She never learns.

"Eden, hey."

"Uh, come on in," I say. I walk away from him and the open door and wave my hand toward the table and chairs in the little kitchenette. "Want to sit?"

"Shit," he says, but then he covers his mouth, points at Junie, and mouths, "Sorry. I mean, oh shoot."

I grin at him and shake my head. "It's all right. As hard as I try to keep the language clean, I wouldn't be surprised if this one can spell the F word before preschool."

"That would be impressive." Vito jerks a hand toward the parking lot. "Ma sent over some food. She will kill me if I let it go bad. Be right back." He dashes away, closing the hotel door behind him.

Once he's gone, I heave a huge sigh. God, he's gorgeous. Adorable. Hot. Sweet. How on earth is this man single?

That's when it hits me.

He lives at home with his mother and father. He's, like, really old not to have his own place. My tummy clenches as I think of all the things that are probably weird and broken about him. Maybe he's bad with money and in debt up to his eyeballs. Maybe he's irresponsible or can't cook. He has one dress shirt, for God's sake.

I square my shoulders and take a deep breath. This isn't a date. This is a new friendship. And anytime my instincts start looking for anything more, I'll just remember that he's probably a mama's boy with terrible habits who would make the world's worst partner, lover, husband. That'll keep me from going into overdrive.

"Knock, knock."

I hear his voice call through the door as he raps lightly. I let him in again, but this time, I step back so there's no chance for a second awkward hug. Besides, there's no room to get close to him. He's carrying a brown cardboard box that looks like it weighs twenty pounds.

"What on earth is all this?" I ask.

Vito laughs and lifts a brow at me. "Lunch, dinner, and a hell of a lot of snacks." He sets the box down on the small kitchen table and points to it. "Leave that here. I need to do something first." He looks around the small living room, squinting dramatically. He seems to make eye contact with Juniper but then looks away. He cups his hands around his eyes and squints, then calls out in a loud voice, "Juniper? Juniper? Are you here?"

He strides into the kitchen and opens the dishwasher, then pretends to call into the racks. "Juniper. Juniper?"

While he wanders the extremely small living space of the hotel suite, Juniper lies with her face on the couch cushion and just blinks at this silly goof of a man.

He's playing a game with her that probably every child knows, but it strikes me in a really deep place.

Nathan's never met his daughter. Wanted her gone before she even existed. And this man who's met her once is already playing with her and giving her his time and attention.

I shake my head to clear the confusing feelings and remind myself he's probably a man-child. Don't believe everything you see, I tell myself. He's a gnome. A mama's boy.

"There she is." Vito says, clapping and dropping to his knees. He points to Juniper once he's on her level and waves. "Hiya, kiddo. Remember me? I'm your mama's friend, Vito. Vito," he says again slowly.

"Veeloo," she echoes, a dribble of drool spilling past her lips.

I grab a cloth diaper from her go bag and blot her lips. "Vito, baby," I say, enunciating the T. "Can you say hi?"

She holds out her arms to Vito, and I cock my chin at him. "Is this cool?"

"More than cool," he says. He picks up Juniper, gives her a quick hug, and then sets her on the floor. "I'm going to put some food away, but then maybe we'll have some time to play?"

She waddles after him like one of the children enchanted by the Pied Piper. But I'm no better. I'm in a daze for this man as much as my daughter is. We stand in the kitchen holding hands while we watch Vito get to work.

"It's good you've got all the amenities here," he says as he unloads plastic containers with labels on the lids into the fridge. "Full-sized appliances. So much better than those dorm-sized jobs most hotels give you." Once he's done, he turns the cardboard over, strips the tape from it, and breaks the box down flat. "You got recycling here? I can take this back to my parents' if you don't know."

I watch him make himself at home in my little space and can't quite explain what I'm feeling. In all the time I was with Nathan, he came to my place hundreds of times. We ate out, brought home leftovers, and he never once so much as remembered to bring leftovers in from the car, let alone put anything in my fridge. He wouldn't even help himself to a glass of water.

To be fair, he never stayed more than a couple of hours. Never a whole night. But I don't know how to feel about Vito showing up and just being so at ease.

It's like he's comfortable in my life and with me, and there's nothing new or awkward about this.

But he doesn't give me a lot of time to process or think.

As if he read my thoughts, he opens a cabinet,

grabs a drinking glass, and helps himself to a glass of water from the tap. "You want something?" he asks, as though proving he is the opposite of the kind of man I've known before. He might as well be named Not Nathan.

"No. I'm good, thanks," I manage, picking up my daughter and holding her close. I don't like to use her to comfort me, but I could go for a little comfort. But Junie knows what she wants, and she is excited about her new friend.

She wiggles out of my arms and toddles over to Vito before grabbing on to the leg of his jeans.

He sips the water, then sets the glass on the counter. "All right, ladies. What do we got?"

He's looking at me expectantly, and I honestly have no idea what he's talking about. I'm struck speechless by the fact that he's come into my hotel room, made himself at home, and now, he's picked up my daughter and is bouncing her on his hip.

"Eden?" he asks, giving me a confused look. "Everything all right?"

"How are you so good at this?" I ask, not even trying to mask the sound of my confusion.

"Kids?" he asks, sounding equally surprised. "I'm one of four kids, and in the last two years, I've become an uncle to four kids."

I nod. "Yeah, I remember, but a lot of people have siblings and kids in their family. You're, like, really good at this."

"It's in the genes," he says, his voice low. "I come by it naturally. I love kids. Love people, honestly. I'm easygoing. You have to be when you're a Bianchi." He grows quiet for a moment, as if he's thinking. "Have you been around a lot of people who are not good at this?"

I swallow hard and murmur, "Yeah. You could say that."

Vito taps Junie on the nose and grins big at both of us. "Well, ladies, you're in for a treat today."

CHAPTER 5
VITO

EDEN PULLS out some toys to keep Juniper entertained while we sit knee-to-knee at her kitchen table poring over the listings on her phone.

"So, the agent sent me six," she says. She's leaning toward me, holding her phone in one hand, but it takes all my concentration to look at the pictures and not at the generous amount of cleavage I can see when she leans closer to me.

Eden Byrne is gorgeous. Her hair is long, and the loose curls practically float over her shoulders. Her eyes are a perfect shade of coffee brown.

Every time she leans closer, I catch a whiff of something light but so elegant. She smells expensive, like the luxury spas Michelle used to treat herself to. What I can't figure out is this girl's story.

"I really like these," she says, flipping the display to reveal a couple of houses that would be way out of my price range. "But then, Taylor sent over this one too. It looks older, but it's the cheapest on the list, so I thought it would be worth seeing."

"Oh fuck," I say before I can stop myself. I look toward Juniper, but she seems engrossed in her magnets. "Sorry about that."

"What is it?" she asks. "Something about this house? Was there a fire or something?"

I shake my head and take the phone from her hands, letting my fingertips just graze hers. Heat flows from her hand through my body, and I'm suddenly feeling about ten degrees hotter.

"No fire," I explain. I zoom into the listing to confirm the address. "I know this house." A little sadness jerks at my chest just looking at the place. "I haven't been there in a while," I say. I hand the phone to her. "My ex-wife's grandfather lives there. I hear he's been moved into a memory care facility across town. They must be selling the house."

I'm quiet for a moment because the thought of Michelle's gramps not being able to live in his house anymore is damn sad. I hope the day never comes when we have to make that decision for our parents.

But then I remind myself that Michelle's parents should be the ones dealing with this, not her, but that's a fight I gave up on long ago.

I meet Eden's eyes. "It's a great house," I tell her. "Solid construction. The old man took good care of the place. Real good. But unless the family's done something in the last five years, and I'm guessing by that purchase price they haven't, the interior needs a gut rehab. If you're in the market for a fixer-upper, that'd be a safe investment. But if you want move-in ready…"

Eden is quiet, but then she shocks the shit out of me by resting a hand over mine. Her touch is light and soft. "You're divorced?" she asks. "I had no idea. I'm so sorry."

I can't tell from her tone if she thinks I'm still nursing a broken heart or if she's digging a little for dirt. I hope it's that second one.

"Yeah," I say. "My marriage was like your bathroom fire. Hot, wild, and over almost before it really got going."

Eden yanks her hand away and covers her mouth with a hand as she blurts out a laugh. "Vito." She shakes her head. "You're so unexpected."

I grin at her. "Well, it's true. I'll tell the story. I

ain't shy about it." I cross my arms over my chest and kick my legs out in front of me. "I was a twenty-six-year-old hothead," I start out, setting the scene for her. "I'm fighting fires by day, and at night, well, let's just say I'm spending a lot of my nights off at The Body Shop. You know the place?"

She shakes her head. "What is it? A fragrance store? Candles and soaps and stuff?"

I crack a laugh. "Nah. We've got two Body Shops in Star Falls. The one where my sister works is a tattoo shop. Gracie, you met her, is an artist and the owner. My ex danced at the other place, under a stage name Exotic."

I watch as the emotions flicker across Eden's face. Confusion, recognition, and then understanding.

"You married a dancer?" she asks.

I watch the flush creep up her neck. "It's totally fine to say I married a stripper. I knew what she did for work, and I didn't give a damn how she made her living. She didn't do anything more than dance, even though I know she got offers, but she had big dreams. She wasn't about to have a criminal record hold her back." I think back on the good times I had with my ex-wife, and I have to admit that.

She wasn't bad at all until, of course, she decided to dance her way across my heart and out of my life.

"We dated for two years, got married on a whim, and split one year later. And that was that." I look down at my hands. I'm fine talking about it, but it seems weird to tell this woman who I'm just getting to know—and feeling no small amount of attraction to—that I was heartbroken when my marriage split up. "I loved her," I admit. "But I learned pretty fast, love isn't enough. Not to make a marriage work, that is. Funny, isn't it? I guess families are the same too. I love my parents, brothers, and Gracie. And that love is enough. It can be too much sometimes. But that's why I moved back in with my parents after the divorce. The world didn't feel right without people around me who I could trust and count on."

Eden is quiet, and I wonder if I'm bringing her down.

I tap my fingers against the table and motion toward the phone. "So, yeah, you want my ex's grandfather's house, put it on the list."

She reaches across the tiny space that separates us and covers my hands with hers. "I'm so sorry if seeing that house brings back painful memories. There's no way I'd take you there even if I did want it. But I don't. I don't have it in me to rehab a house." She nods toward Juniper. "She's a very easy baby, but no baby is easy enough to raise in a construction zone." She squeezes my hands and then releases them. "Thanks for sharing all that, Vito."

I nod, not sure what else to say. Almost everyone in town knows my history with Michelle. It's been a long time since I talked about it. It almost feels good to. "Thanks for listening," I tell her. "And not judging me. I married for the right reasons. I just picked the wrong person."

My words hang between us, and a slight shift charges the air between us.

"So," she says, swiping at her touchscreen. "What do you think about a ranch versus a two-story?"

I offer to drive so Eden can look over the neighborhoods, the streets, even scanning for parks and things as we drive to each of the houses that have been set up.

"Want to take my car?" she asks, bending down to lift Juniper into her arms.

I look away from the view of her cleavage, but only after I get a nice eyeful. I'm respectful, but hell, Eden's body is something straight out of my fantasies. I never thought of myself as a guy with a type before. I've dated skinny, toned women like my ex, women with a little extra junk in their trunk, tall, thin, dark, light. I don't discriminate. But I also don't ever stick around and get too close. Not since Michelle, at least. But if I did have a type, tall and lush with a rack I could bury my face in would be it, and that's Eden.

Fuck.

I'd better concentrate on inspecting properties for hazards. Not inspecting Eden's smoking-hot curves and dreaming of touching her.

"Vito?" She meets my eyes, and I snap my wandering thoughts back to her.

"Sorry," I say. "Ready to go?"

She follows me out the door, giving me a sexy smile as I wait for the hotel door to close behind us. Then, I turn and test the handle to make sure the electronic safety has engaged, and the door is actually locked.

"You always like this?" she asks, accepting my silent offer to take the diaper bag from her.

"Like what?" I ask.

She is studying my face over the top of Juniper's curly hair. "Attentive," she finally says. "Thoughtful. Maybe safety-conscious?"

I shrug. "I don't think anyone in my line of work can avoid it."

She grows quiet, and I follow her to a brand-new

SUV with Ohio plates. "I'm sure," she says softly. "Do you mind driving my car? It's a pain installing the car seat over and over."

I laugh out loud at that and lean maybe a little too close to her. "You realize that's one of the services we offer?"

She looks confused for a second but then bursts out laughing. "Is that true? Do people really come down to the fire station to make sure their car seats are safely installed?"

"All the time." I hold open the rear passenger door while Eden secures Juniper in the seat.

"I don't know why I thought that wasn't really a thing," she chuckles. After Juniper is buckled in, Eden turns to me and extends the hand holding the keys. "You sure you don't mind?"

I take the keys, and I'm damn sure she almost clasps my hands as she passes over an efficient silver ring with just one simple key fob for the car on it. It startles me a little when I realize she doesn't have any other keys. No place to call home that requires keys. The hotel has cards for entry. She just lost her rental home. As far as I know, she has no job, but she does have money. I have so many questions about this woman.

I do my best to shake off the quick brush of her soft skin as I take the fob. I roll my shoulders and hold open the passenger door so she can slide in. Once I'm settled and my seat belt is secured, I look back at Juniper. "Everybody ready?"

Juniper is smashing a plush rabbit against her knees, and of course she's securely belted in. Eden is too, so I adjust the mirrors and punch the address of the first house into my phone even though I don't really need it.

"Fancy," I say, grinning as I plug my phone into the loose cable that connects my device to her car. "Your in-dash display is bigger than my parents' television."

It's a joke, and she laughs, which I love. She may have money, but she's not weird about it. Which is great. I don't give a shit if she's got two cents to her name. A woman with a sense of humor and a low-key attitude is worth her weight in gold.

As we drive, I point out the schools and parks and other little points of interest. Star Falls is a great place to live. Great people, beautiful land, big sky. I love it here, and it must show.

"You sound like an official tour guide," she says, but there's a smile in her voice.

"Small-town living," I tell her. "Can't beat it."

She's quiet, staring out the window as we turn onto the street where the first house is. I know the area, but I don't see a for-sale sign in any of the lawns or front windows, so I slow down to a crawl.

"Did you ever live anyplace else? Ever want to live someplace bigger?"

"Like Los Angeles?" I ask but don't give her time to reply. "Nah." I wrinkle my nose. But then I stop and really think about it. Something about her makes me want to dig a little deeper. Give her more of me. "Let me rephrase that. I would absolutely consider moving away from Star Falls for the right reason. I actually applied for a job at a bigger firehouse about a month ago."

"Yeah?" She turns fully in her seat to look at me, but then Juniper starts fussing. "We're almost there, honey." Eden turns in her seat to pick up the bunny that's somehow been slingshotted deep behind the driver's seat. She bends and twists, and I keep my eyes on the damn road, refusing to ogle her while she's picking up her baby's toy.

Once Eden has the bunny, Juniper stops squirming, and I see a for sale sign up ahead about another half block away.

"That looks like our stop," I tell her. "Juniper, we're almost there. You ready to look at a new house?

"Yah, yah, yah." In her excitement, she throws the bunny again, and it must land behind me, because Eden shakes her head and blows air through her lips.

"Baby, we're about to get out of the car. I'll get your bunny in a sec," Eden tells her.

Juniper seems fine with that, so as I find a place to park on the street near the property, Eden asks me a gentle question. "But you didn't get the job? Or you did and didn't take it?"

"Didn't get it," I say simply. "I'll tell you what happened on the way to the next house. If you want to hear the boring story."

She nods, and I kill the ignition and offer the key back to her.

"You hang on to it," she says. "As long as you don't mind driving to the next place?"

I nod and jump out of the car. I run around and open the door for her, then stand by while she gets Juniper out of the back.

"Ready?" I ask, locking the car and slipping the fob into the pocket of my jeans. "This could be your new home."

She looks nervous but excited, and she nods

73

vigorously. "I'm so glad you came. Thanks for being here."

A wave of sweet warmth floods my chest at her words, but I just urge her ahead. "Come on," I tell her.

We walk up the drive, but we don't even make it to the front door when a very stressed-looking woman meets us.

"Eden?" She's waving her hand and trotting down the concrete driveway in ridiculously high heels. As she meets us, I can't help noticing that even in heels, she's like six inches shorter than Eden.

"Hi, Taylor." Eden secures Juniper on one hip. Since I have the diaper bag, she's got a free hand to shake the real estate agent's hand.

"So nice to finally meet you," she says to Eden before turning her attention toward me. "You must be Dad." She extends her hand.

I chuckle and Eden's about to say something, but I shake the lady's hand. "What gave me away?"

I'm not trying to horn in on Eden's party or nothing, but if the real estate lady thinks there's a man in the picture, who knows. Maybe the sellers will be more reasonable if they think some happy couples about to buy their dream home.

Taylor steps a little closer to us and lowers her

voice. Her bright-pink lipstick has smeared onto her front teeth, and she's got a light sheen of sweat on her forehead. "I hope this won't make you uncomfortable." She tosses a look behind her toward the open front door of the house. "The homeowner was supposed to leave to let you view the place privately. It's something we ask, but this homeowner won't go."

I look at Eden for guidance on this. "You want to pass?"

She bites her lower lip. "It's really cute," she says. "I'd like to see it. Do you think it'll be too awkward?"

"We're fine. Eden wants to see this house, she's going to see the house. It doesn't bother us that the man is home."

I look at Eden. "You good?"

She's looking at me with the cutest expression of shock and something I can't make out. But she nods.

"Excellent," I say. "Ms. Taylor, you good?"

"I'm fantastic," she says, looking relieved.

"Then if this one's ready," I say, lifting a brow at Juniper, "then we're solid. Let's see this house."

The real estate lady turns on her super-high heels and rushes ahead of us toward the house. "Mr. Incandella," she calls. "The family is here."

As I start to follow her up the drive, Eden rests a hand on my elbow. "Vito," she says, those melted-chocolate eyes boring into mine. "I told her you were just a friend. I'm sorry about that. I think she just assumed."

I chuckle. "You think I care that she thought I had something to do with this?" I jerk a thumb at Juniper. "I'm freaking flattered. Now, come on. Let's see this house."

CHAPTER 6
EDEN

THE SECOND we walk into the house, the homeowner appears wearing the world's most aggressive scowl. I'm taken aback, honestly. He looks angry, and unless he's being forced to sell his home for financial reasons, I can't imagine why he'd greet a prospective buyer looking like he's about to go off on us.

"Uh, hi," I say, "I'm Eden. Thank you so much for making time to see us today."

I hold out my hand, but he looks from me to Vito and then back at my hand. Then he reaches out and shakes mine. "Robert," he says.

Vito shakes his hand too, but stays quiet, letting me do the talking. I'm asking how long he's lived here and wondering why Taylor isn't saying anything. Suddenly, I see Vito shift from one foot to the other.

"Do you mind if I take off my shoes?" Vito asks. "My mother would send me to my room without dinner if I wore my shoes in the house."

Taylor looks mortified, but immediately the homeowner's shoulders soften a bit. I look down at his feet and see he's wearing socks with pristine-looking open-toed house slippers just like the ones I saw Vito wearing the day we met.

"Well, if it's all the same to you," Robert says, "I'd appreciate that. My wife...my, uh, late wife felt the same about shoes as your mother."

Taylor tries to get out of her shoes so fast, she nearly tips over. She has to hold on to the wall to wrench her bare feet out of those heels, but she does it, and she finishes just as Vito gets his running shoes off.

He's wearing the most hilarious socks, and I nearly snort. They must have been some kind of gift. I watch him walk up to me, staring at the truly ridiculous sight of a small Chihuahua lifting its leg to pee on a fire hydrant. I'm not sure if they're making some kind of statement, but the socks keep me from being too distracted as the hunky firefighter comes close.

Without saying a word, Vito points at Juniper's

super-soft baby slippers. "Come on, kid. This is another one of those no-shoes places. Don't make a scene."

The homeowner, Robert, actually cracks a half smile at that and gives Juniper a wave. "Hello, there."

He seems awkward with her, so maybe not a grandpa himself, but I go through the motions and tug off her shoes and hand them to Vito. He tucks them into his back pocket, and then he holds out his hands for my daughter and, without a word, nods at me.

I hand him my baby and toe out of my shoes. Once we're all out of our shoes, Robert steps aside and lets the real estate agent bring us into the kitchen.

There is a glossy, full-color listing sheet on the marble countertop, and she starts right in, pointing out features of the home and comparing what we can see around us to the stats on the printout.

Vito hands Juniper back to me and stands by quietly with Robert while Taylor shows me the new fridge, the oven, and the double sink.

"The kitchen was rehabbed just two years ago," Taylor says. She's droning on about the appliances being energy efficient, but I stop listening. I'm in love with this kitchen. It's like the designer of my dreams put this place together. You can tell by the layout that the original kitchen was designed for a family. A built-in table with bench-style seats is in a nook on the rear wall of the kitchen and is surrounded by windows that look out onto a fenced backyard.

The counters are white marble with wisps of bronze-gold running through them. The cabinets are a rustic-looking dark wood with matching bronze pulls, and the floors are a lighter wood than the cabinets, likely original but in great shape. The appliances are all stainless steel, which you'd think would clash with the bronze of the hardware, but I don't care. This kitchen has tons of counter space and light. There's even a little window box that could hold plants over the large farmhouse-style sink.

I walk up to the sink and run my hand over the pristine porcelain. "This sink is so big, I could give Juniper a bath in there."

Junie leans out of my arms, trying to turn on the faucet, and I don't try to stop her. I grab the handle to test the water pressure, and to my delight, the fixture has several settings to adjust how much water comes out.

I know better than to act like I'm in love with this place in the very first room, so I look closely at every-thing I can. I flick the switches and watch the lights come on. I peek inside the fridge and oven... Sadly, they seem brand-new.

"Have these ever been used?" I ask Taylor quietly.

Robert's just asked Vito what he does for a living, so Taylor seems a little more relaxed talking with the homeowner distracted.

She leans in close and says, "I don't think he cooks much."

I nod, wondering why on earth he'd put in such a gorgeous kitchen and not use it, but then I remember he mentioned a late wife, and my stomach tightens.

I don't ask anything more and follow Taylor's lead. She shows us the downstairs powder room, and Vito takes a look under the sink and lifts the lid off the toilet tank. He flushes the toilet once, then looks up at me with a sweet, wide smile.

"Nothing to report, chief," he says. "Carry on."

He and Robert haven't stopped talking about the house and safety issues since Vito revealed he's a fire-fighter, so I guess that could be a good thing.

The house has a dining room to the right of the entryway. We passed it to go toward the kitchen, and we head back there after I see the laundry room and the powder room. The dining room is a little empty of furniture and pictures, which seems a bit odd, but the size is fine. We walk past the staircase and front door to the left, coming to a family room that is open to the kitchen. The family room has a fireplace, and it's clear there's been some more renovation here.

"This was originally a Georgian," Taylor explains, "so the living room off the kitchen had that wall to keep it separate. But the family room has been renovated to open up the floor plan a bit. Permits were pulled, of course. The home passed all its inspections, and only licensed contractors were used."

There was a time when I might not have cared at all about that, but after the fire in the rental house, I'm relieved to hear that things were done to code here. I flick a glance at Vito, who looks like he's half listening to me, half listening to Robert. He lifts his eyebrows at me as if to ask how I'm liking it, and I give a short nod, trying not to give too much away.

He slowly nods back, all casual and chill so that it looks like he's just mulling over something Robert has said.

Our little nonverbal exchange prickles the hairs on my arms. The easy intimacy with this man makes me wonder what else could feel easy and right with him.

"There are four bedrooms," Taylor says loudly, dragging my attention away from Vito. "And two full baths. Shall we take a look?"

This is the biggest of the homes that we're looking at today. Four bedrooms, two full baths upstairs and the powder room downstairs. There's a basement, a backyard, and a garage.

As we take the carpeted stairs, I realize that moving to Ohio was a really smart move financially.

The upstairs of this place could be a house of horrors, but based on that kitchen alone, I already know the truth in my heart. I want it. This is a place I could make a home for Junie and me. I can just imagine a dog running in the fenced yard, breakfasts at that eat-in area. I haven't had holidays in the Midwest before, so picturing the leaves changing, snow drifting over the thick limbs of the mature trees...

My heart rate starts to pick up, and I begin to grin uncontrollably. For the first time since I got pregnant, I feel like I can have fun with my life. I have a little money. I have a beautiful baby. I might have a house.

After everything I've been through on my own these last couple of years, I am beginning to see a path to something that feels real. That feels like mine.

I can't stop myself from looking over at Vito and imagining him being here with me. Not just for support. Waking up with him. Washing dishes with him beside me.

A sudden flush creeps up my neck, and I have to wave my hand in front of my face to cool off. That kind of thinking is way too much. We're just friends, and barely that. And with my track record, a new house is more than enough reality to manage.

I clutch Junie tighter and follow Taylor's perfectly pedicured toes up the stairs.

When we hit the landing at the top, Vito rests a light hand against my lower back. "You want me to carry her?" he asks. "You look flushed."

I shake my head and sputter, "I'm good." I've got to put some distance between him and me.

I follow Taylor into the bathroom at the top of the stairs. I'm half tempted to splash cold water on myself, but I don't.

I clear my throat and push past Vito's stupidly sexy arm, which he's using to lean against the bathroom door.

"Master bedroom?" I ask, using every ounce of willpower not to think about the fact that the master bedroom is going to have a nice, big, beautiful bed.

By the time we've finished the walk-through, Robert and Vito are talking in the driveway. Robert is pointing up at the roof, and Vito's got a pair of sunglasses covering his face. He's looking up where

Robert is gesturing, which I hope means he's trying to point out something about the roof that's positive, like it's been repaired or replaced recently.

"So," Taylor asks, placing her heels back on as I'm setting Junie on the tile foyer floor while I slip my shoes back on. Taylor's grin is huge, and she lowers her voice. "What do you think? Did you like it? Is this a place you could see living with your family?"

My heart catches in my throat at her question. Even though I told her that Vito is just a friend, I'm sure she's not really interested in the specifics. She just wants to know if I'm interested enough to make an offer on the house.

I think through everything I saw. The bathrooms, the basement, the yard. "The upstairs bathrooms have not been renovated," I tell her, "but they have been well maintained. Eventually, they'll need some work."

Taylor nods, a shadow covering her bright expression. "True, but that's why the house is in your price range," she says. "If the upstairs bathrooms had been updated..." She makes a whooshing sound with her lips. "That would up the purchase price by a bunch."

I know she's telling the truth, so I decide to be

honest with her as well. "I'd like to see the other houses on the list before I make any decisions."

"Oh my gosh, yes," she says, holding the screen door open for me. "We'll see as many houses as you need. Buying a house is a lot like finding the perfect wedding dress. More often than not, the first one is usually it. But you need to see what else is out there to be sure. This is a big decision, and you need to be certain."

I've never bought a wedding dress. Never even shopped for one. My high school best friend and I had a major falling-out right before her wedding. That was right around the time that everything went down with my mom. I'm ashamed to admit it, but I backed out of being in her wedding, and we haven't spoken since.

"I wouldn't know about the wedding dress," I say quietly. "But I know what you mean."

As we walk down the concrete driveway, my heart rate picks up when Vito lowers his face from looking up at the roof to face me. I'm saying the words before I can even stop them. "I'd like to hear what Vito thought, too."

"Absolutely," Taylor says. But then she looks a little confused. "But it will be just you and the little one? You'll be making the purchase alone, correct?"

I nod in answer to her question, but I pick up the pace when Vito grins and waves me over. When Junie and I reach him, Vito jerks a thumb toward Robert.

"So," Vito says, tugging the sunglasses from his face. "Robert worked at the same mill as my pops. But he was management and Pops was on the floor, so they didn't overlap much." Vito turns to the homeowner and claps his new friend on the shoulder. "Good people," he says warmly. "And this house?" Vito looks me right in the eye and nods. "Passed my inspection. How about yours?"

Just as I'm about to answer, the worst stench wafts up, and I wrinkle my nose. "Oh no," I say. "I think I need to change a diaper." I look from the homeowner to Taylor. "Thank you for showing me the house. If you'll excuse me, I'm going to take this mess to my truck."

Vito fishes my keys out of his pocket. "Want help?" he asks. "I'll be right behind you." He turns and extends a hand to the homeowner, whose face is contorted in a grimace.

"You're going to do that where?" Robert asks. "In the car?"

I nod and shrug. "I have hand sanitizer in my bag, and we'll toss the mess in a trash bin someplace. I'm used to this."

He shakes his head. "But where do you lay the baby?"

"I keep a changing pad in this bag. It's not a problem."

Robert frowns as he looks at Vito. For a second, I feel a little defensive that he's talking to him instead of me, but when I hear what he says, my heart melts a little. "Would it be better to change the baby inside? Any reason she couldn't do it in the upstairs bathroom? I don't mind if you use the towels." He swallows, and a shimmer of tears seems to redden his eyes. "That sink could probably use somebody running the water."

Vito turns to me and lifts his brows. "Eden? Want to use the upstairs bathroom?" He tips his chin a bit and then adds, "I wouldn't mind chatting with Robert a few more minutes."

To be honest, I've changed Junie's diapers on my lap, in the grocery store, on park benches. Taking care of business in the car is no big deal at all, but something about the kind offer from Robert and Vito's encouragement makes it impossible to say no. I'll take a sink and a fluffy bathmat over the changing pad and the back seat any day.

"I'll go with you." Taylor looks like never in all her days of real estate agenting has something like this happened, so I reassure her it'll just take a second.

Junie starts to whine and squirm, so I follow Taylor inside. I kick off my shoes, and Taylor pulls out her phone. "Go on up," she tells me. "I'm going to check my email."

I pad upstairs with Junie and, for a moment, let myself imagine this is my house. We walk into the bathroom, close the door behind us, and make quick work of changing her diaper. I'm a pro at it after thousands of dirty ones.

Since the door is closed, I let Junie crawl on the floor while I wash my hands and dry them on the hand towel.

When we make it back downstairs, Taylor's smile is bright, and she looks surprised. "That was quick. See you at the next house? It's only about a half mile away, so it shouldn't take long to get there."

I nod and head back down the driveway. "All set," I call out. "Robert, I used the hand towel upstairs, but everything else should be exactly as I found it."

The garage is open, and Robert points to a pristine-looking black plastic bin. He grimaces. "Please," he says. "Toss it in there."

I shake my head. "Oh no. You don't want this

hanging around until your next trash pickup. We'll dispose of it along the way. No problem."

Robert shakes his head again. "Please. I insist." He looks at Vito and smiles a little. "The garage is very well insulated. I haven't smelled my trash in thirty-two years in this house. I don't expect one little diaper to change that."

Vito lifts his brows. "All due respect, but I've got a nephew about her age. There ain't nothing quite like the smell of baby shit."

The homeowner laughs and actually puts a hand on Vito's shoulders. "I'll take your word for it. But go on. I don't mind."

Vito holds a hand out to me, takes the small bag with the diaper from me, and throws it in the bin, then firmly secures the lid in place. When he turns back around, he holds his other hand out to Robert, and they shake, exchanging a few quiet words.

I wave to the homeowner as I follow Vito to my SUV.

I don't say anything while I buckle Juniper into her seat. I'm quiet as Vito comes around, holds open my door, and waits while I get settled in the passenger seat. But Vito is all smiles and chatter as he twists in his seat and confirms that everybody's ready to go.

"Hey, is that bunny buckled?" He's leaning over

the middle console pointing at Juniper's stuffed animal, when I reach for his arm.

He turns in the seat and faces me. "You all good?" he asks. His chin is covered in dusky stubble, like he skipped shaving today. I know I have made terrible decisions when it comes to men, but when I see the curve at the corner of his mouth, the way his cheek dimples ever so slightly…it all just hits me.

The warmth of the SUV, the smell of the new leather, and the richness of his cologne.

"You," I murmur, shaking my head. "What you…"

Whether it's my body talking or my heart or the brain that I can never trust to make the right decisions at times like these, I have to get closer to him. Before I can deny the impulse and talk myself into behaving rationally, I lean forward and cup his chin. His sunglasses are on the top of his perfectly waved hair, his deep brown eyes wide as he scans my face.

His expression changes. He stares without blinking and lowers his chin, almost nuzzling against my palm.

"Eden?" he says, his voice thick and low.

"Vito." And before I can stop myself, I lean in to kiss him.

CHAPTER 7
VITO

I DON'T HAVE time to react before Eden's lips brush across mine. Her mouth is soft as it opens against mine. Her fingers tighten, and a breathy little sigh rumbles in her throat, the sound so fucking hot, it's like someone hit the on switch in my balls. My cock literally jerks in my jeans, but before I even realize it's happening, it's over.

Eden pulls back like she's been shocked and covers her mouth with a hand. "Oh shit. Shit, shit," she mutters. "I am so sorry. I should not have done that."

I reach across the console and tug one of her hands from her face. I lace my fingers through hers and give her a squeeze. "I'm going to stop you right there," I say. "You have nothing to apologize for."

"No, no, I do," she says, her words coming out in a rush. "I don't even know why I did that. I mean…I do know. I just…" She seems to notice that I'm holding her hand, and she lets her other hand drop down to trace my knuckles. "You're not mad?"

I laugh and squeeze her hand. "Babe, I don't know what the guys in LA are like, but if what you're looking for is an invitation or permission or some shit…" I flick a look back at Junie and realize we've both been cussing up a storm. "Or some stuff," I correct, "you got it. You need me to say yes, you got your yes."

"Yeah?" she asks, seeming to calm down a little. She laughs softly as her shoulders relax. "I was more concerned that maybe you weren't…"

I turn in my seat to look at her. "Maybe I wasn't what?"

My eyes travel from her flushed cheeks along the deep vee in the long-sleeved top she's wearing under a light, loose cardigan. Her thighs are painted into the dark jeans she's wearing, and all I can think about is peeling away that fabric and the smooth skin of those thighs clamped around my ears while she rides my face.

"Interested?" I growl. "Attracted?" I shift around in my seat to relieve some of the pressure that's building up from the partial boner that kiss gave me. Fuck, not just the kiss. It's Eden. Her body. Her personality. "If you hadn't ended that kiss so fast, we'd be halfway to making Juniper a sibling right now."

Her laugh is nervous as I turn on the ignition and set the GPS to the next address. I meet Eden's gaze, and we trade grins. Any asshole with eyes can tell Eden is stunning, so I'm guessing she's hesitating because she's been treated like shit in the past. Most women I know have asshole men stories that could fill a library.

Now seems about as good a time as any to ask.

"So," I start. We're just a few minutes from the next house. Not a ton of time to bring up serious shit, but we can at least put a pin in it and continue the conversation later. If it's something she's even up to sharing. "Eden, you know you're smokin' hot, stacked, beautiful. I ain't got the vocabulary to come up with more words, but you're it," I say on a grin. "So, I take it the donor did you dirty?"

"The donor?" she asks, but then she seems to get it. "You mean Juniper's dad?" She flicks a look over her shoulder and smiles at the little girl playing happily with her bunny. "Yeah, that's a story, and thanks, by the way. For the compliments. I don't think

I've been called stacked before. At least, not that I ever remember."

"I meant that in the best possible way," I tell her. "And I love stories." We'll be at the next house in like six minutes. "But if it's not a short one, it might have to wait." I nod at the display on her truck that shows the map and that we're almost to the destination.

I see her shift in the passenger seat. "It's kind of a long story, and there are parts of it I..." She sighs. "It's effed up, Vito. Really effed up. I want to share it, but be warned, you might not like what you hear. You might not even like me once you hear it."

"Please," I scoff. "There's nothing you can say that would make me feel any differently about you."

"I haven't made the best decisions in life," she says as she slides out of the car when I park, trying to avoid the conversation. I hope this conversation isn't over because I want to know everything she seems so scared to share.

I go around and grab the diaper bag and sling it over my shoulder. "I know one thing that might help," I offer.

Once she's got Juniper in her arms, I click the fob to lock the car and slip the keys back into my pocket.

She smooths Juniper's hair with a hand but peeks over her baby's head to meet my eyes. "Yeah?" she asks, a small smile playing on those perfect lips. "What's that?"

"When it comes to what you did in the car back there," I say, grinning, "your gut was right on. Maybe before, you trusted your feelings, but you just couldn't trust the person you had the feelings for."

Her lips part, and she looks at me with an expression that's part sad, part thankful. "I think that first house was the one, but I still want to look at a few more to be sure."

Something in her voice gives me the feeling she is talking about more than just the house. "When you know, you know," I assure her, resting my palm lightly against her lower back. "And if it's really the one for you, it'll be there when you're ready. Now, I think I see what looks like some very filthy gutters." I point to the roof of the house ahead of us. "Not liking this one already, but let's take a look. Maybe we'll find some proof that your gut is right and you've already found the one."

By the time we finish looking at every house on the list, it's a lot later than I expected. In the driveway of the last house, Juniper has a full meltdown. She's eaten snacks from the diaper bag, had water and another diaper change, but even Eden looks a little tired and flustered.

"I'm starving," she says. "And you've got to be too." She looks at her watch and bounces Juniper against her hip. "I'd wanted to make one more stop before going back to the hotel, but I don't think Junie's got it in her. Do you mind if we head back?"

My stomach growls. "Can we stop for some food along the way?"

She nods, thanks Taylor for all the work today, and then bustles off toward the SUV.

I click the fob to unlock the vehicle and turn to shake Taylor's hand. "Thanks for letting me tag along," I say. "It was nice meeting you." I'm turning to head out when Taylor calls my name.

"Vito," she says, then looks toward Eden, who is coaxing a very cranky baby into her car seat. "I think Eden really liked that first house. What do you think?"

I nod. "It's her call, but no doubt that house will make a great home. Well maintained, move-in condition. Upstairs bathrooms could use a remodel at some point, but nothing she couldn't live with for a couple years. If she makes a decision, I'm sure she'll let you know."

Taylor nods. "A house like that won't stay on the market long." I'm not sure why she's telling me this, but then, of course, she drops the bomb. "You know, if your credit is an issue, we have programs. I work with a lot of mortgage brokers, and we'll find a way. There's no reason why the two of you can't make this happen."

I bark out a laugh. "Thanks for that," I say. "But my credit's just fine, not that it matters since I won't be buying the house. But I'll pass that along to Eden."

Taylor looks confused, like even though Eden said we were just friends, she doesn't believe I won't be moving in to the house with her. But she just says okay and shoves a handful of business cards at me. I didn't think people used business cards much anymore, but I take them, thank her again, and head over to the truck.

Juniper is in full scream mode, with tears on her red face and her lower lip trembling, coated with drool, she's so worked up.

I've seen epic meltdowns like this before, so I know the best thing to do is let Mom tell me what she wants. I press my hand to Eden's lower back. "Can I help?" I ask. "Jokes? Take her for a walk? We don't need to get in the car right now. Whatever she needs, we do."

Eden looks at me with gratitude all over her face. She looks flustered too. "Thanks," she says, "but I think she's tired. I should have paid closer attention to the time. We missed her nap by about an hour. I'm going to ride in the back with her if you don't mind playing chauffeur."

"Absolutely. Go around. I'll hang with her until you're in."

While Eden runs around the rear bumper to climb into the seat behind the driver, I look down at sad little Juniper. My heart tightens physically in my chest at the misery on her cute face. She's obviously worked up and overtired if she missed her nap, but I can't help wanting to do something.

"Hey, kiddo," I say, reaching a hand out to her. I don't do anything, just reach my fingers toward her, and Juniper surprises me by lifting her arms up and screaming a very easy-to-understand word.

"Up. Up."

I look helplessly at Eden, who is climbing into the back seat. "What do I do?" I ask. "She wants up?"

Eden sighs. "Yeah, I'm sure she does." She looks at Taylor, who's staring at us through the window, and waves. "You know what, get her up. She's had a long day, and she's wrecked. Maybe she'll calm down a bit if we just let her settle."

With Juniper continuing to scream, I reach into the back seat, unbuckle her safety belt, and pick her up from the car seat. She flops against my shoulder, her little mouth biting into my shirt.

"Oh God." When Eden comes around and sees Juniper's basically gone vampire on me, she runs back to the car for the diaper bag. "Teething," she says. "Poor kiddo. I'll bet she's in pain." She comes back to the passenger side of the car with a little plastic bottle in her hands. "These are organic teething tablets. They'll dissolve against her gums and give her a little relief. Can you hold her while I do this?"

"Yep." I've seen this before, but never up close and personal. It's actually really heartbreaking. She's got to be in some kind of pain, but the second her mom puts her fingers in Junie's mouth, the crying eases. A little white froth bubbles on her lips, but true to Eden's prediction, just having some fingers to bite on seems to calm Juniper down enough to stop the screaming.

"There we go," I say, keeping my voice calm and cheerful. "You got this, kiddo."

Once Juniper seems a little more settled, Eden takes her from me. "I'm going to walk a sec," she says.

She takes off at a nice brisk pace down the side-walk, patting Juniper's back and letting her grind her mouth against her shoulder like she did to me. I close the doors, lock the car, and catch up to them, walking alongside Eden. We don't say anything; I just keep pace while she coos to her daughter.

"Good way to check out the neighborhood," she says, throwing me a look. "I'm sorry, Vito. I know we're both starving. What a disaster."

I shake my head. "This has been a pretty perfect day in my book," I say. "No fires, no MVAs. I think I can handle running support on a teething meltdown."

"MVA?" she echoes.

"Motor vehicle accident," I explain.

She nods, and as we approach the end of the third block, Juniper has quieted down a lot. We slow our pace, and by the time we get back to the car, Juniper is almost asleep on Eden's shoulder.

She gently sets her daughter back in the car seat, and I watch as her drowsy eyelids blink fast, her thick eyelashes casting shadows on her cheeks.

I always thought I'd have kids someday. I thought I'd end up having them with Michelle. But I could see being somebody's dad like this. What I can't imagine is giving up on a kid that I have, even if shit didn't work out with the baby momma.

My gut clenches when I think about my divorced friends. My sister's husband is a widower, so she didn't have to navigate any issues with an ex-wife, the birth mother of her stepkids. If anybody could do it, Gracie could.

What if Juniper's father is still in the picture? I don't know how cool I'd be sharing a kid with a deadbeat dad. But before I jump to judgment, I've got to remind myself that not everyone has a family like mine. I don't know if Eden even has parents.

"You mind if I ride in back with her?" Eden's got Juniper strapped in.

I don't reply because of course I don't mind. I wait for her to get in, then I close Juniper's door as Eden gets settled in the back seat, climb behind the wheel, belt in, and head back to Eden's hotel.

"So," I say softly as we're pulling away. "I told you my story. Now a good time for yours?"

Eden chuckles softly. She leans back against the clean leather and closes her eyes. "Take me someplace I can buy you a burger and fries, and I'll tell you anything you want to know."

"Deal," I say, then head toward downtown Star Falls.

CHAPTER 8
EDEN

THE BURGERS from Betta Burger are better than anything I've ever had. The fries are thick, with the skins still on and loads of salt. The patty is perfectly seared but juicy, and the fixings are crisp, fresh, and loaded between a perfectly baked bun.

Vito parked and went inside to order, figuring that the shouting into the drive-through speaker would wake up Junie. He's already finished his burger and fries and is working his way through a peanut butter and chocolate shake while I dip the last of my fries into a tiny dollop of ketchup.

"Come on, you got to taste this." He twists in the driver's seat and holds the cup over the center console. "Just take a sip. I promise I don't have cooties."

I shake my head and think it's already too late for that. I kissed the man just a few minutes ago. It's not a big leap to take a sip from his straw.

I grab the cup and start with a little taste, but I quickly suck down a big mouthful. "Oh my God," I mutter. "What the heck do they put in these? I might have to fight you for the last few sips."

Vito holds his hands up in surrender. "You finish it. I know better than to come between a woman and the best shake in Star Falls."

I take two more long sips and then hand it back to him. "I'm done," I say. "I don't need that much sugar in my life, but that's good."

He slurps the last of the shake then bags up his trash. "I know, right? You need an unofficial tour guide through the best food in Star Falls, I'm your guy."

He holds out a hand, and I give him my burger wrapper and the little waxy bag that has been completely cleaned of any evidence that hand-cut fries were once inside.

Once my belly is full, I lean back against the seat and sigh. "Thank you," I say. "For lunch. For coming with me today. For all of this."

Vito fires up the truck and looks at me in the

rearview. "You bought lunch," he reminds me. "Everything else was my pleasure."

He pulls out of the parking lot of the burger place, and I watch little Junie as she sleeps. Her mouth is open, her lips still shiny with a bit of drool. Thank goodness I have teething toys in the freezer back at the hotel. I have a feeling we're going to need them.

"We got enough time for that story you were going to tell me?" Vito's smiling, but the fact that he's bringing it up again has my stomach suddenly doing flips.

I lace my fingers together and squeeze tight. I can give him the sanitized version of the story I gave my aunt, but I have a feeling he's going to want more. More that I just don't know I can offer. But something about the smirk covering that sexy face loosens my defenses.

I can open up.

Nathan can't hurt me or Junie.

Not as long as I don't break the rules.

"Yeah," I sigh. "Okay. So, my daughter's father… The short version is he wanted nothing to do with a child. When he found out I was pregnant, he was happy to help me solve the problem as long as it had nothing to do with him." I can see in the mirror that

Vito's lips have gone thin, but he looks straight ahead at the road and just listens.

I appreciate that he's not interrupting me with questions or reactions, but I almost wish he would. I'd rather tell him the things he wants to know than just leave me to share, but he's not interrupting so I rush on to fill the silence.

"I told him I was going to have the baby and I planned on keeping her. After that, lawyers got involved, and we worked out an agreement. It's actually pretty unusual." This is where I stop and bite my lip. I told my aunt some of this, but not nearly all there is to tell.

"Okay," he says slowly. "Does he visit her? Get pictures?"

I shake my head. "No, nothing like that." I rub my forehead and suddenly wish we weren't doing this in the car. I'm sitting behind the driver's seat, and it feels like I'm confessing my sins in one of those boxes like I was forced to do for a while in Catholic grade school.

I can't tell how close we are to the hotel because Vito hasn't punched the address into the GPS, so I figure I might as well keep going. If he doesn't want anything to do with me after this, well, it's probably better I know before I go off and kiss the man again.

"Vito," I say quietly. "Some of the details of what happened are sort of confidential. I haven't even told my aunt everything."

He immediately looks into the rearview and meets my eyes. "What do you need me to do? Spit oath? Blood? I was never a Boy Scout, but if there's something I've got to swear to, I'll swear to it. You can trust me with anything, Eden."

The sparkle in his eye makes me giggle. "A spit oath? Is that a thing?"

He cups his palm like he might actually spit in it, but then he grabs the steering wheel. "Fuck if I know. Point is, you can trust me. I've got no reason to tell anybody your business, Eden. The only reason I want to know is so I know whose knees I've got to crack or if I've got to break some bones for you. Some ex shows up you don't want around, some deadbeat bails on child support…" He lifts a thick brow at me. "We Bianchis take care of our own."

We take care of our own…

Am I theirs? His? I have been going to weekly ladies' brunches and hanging out with the Bianchis more than I used to spend time with my friends in LA —if you could really call the people I worked with and occasionally did dinners and happy hours with my friends.

I decide not to think too long about his choice of words but focus on what he's really asking.

"We signed an agreement," I explain. "It's a confidential agreement, which is why I don't talk about it much. Basically, he gave up all parental rights to Juniper in exchange for money. His lawyers set up a fund that will pay me a modest annual income so I can live off the money until she is older. There's also a small amount put away in a separate trust so she can have a head start on college or culinary school, trade school, or just to travel if she wants when she turns eighteen."

He nods slowly but asks only one question. "No parental rights. What does that mean?"

"He's out of her life for good. And mine too. No visits, no emails, no holiday cards."

"He basically bought you off." Vito sounds disgusted. He grumbles something under his breath, and I start to feel too hot.

This was a mistake.

I told him too much, and this isn't even half of it.

"Vito, I know how it sounds."

"Whoa. I'm not judging you, babe." He looks at me in the mirror, his face severe. "You've got a baby to raise, and you're how old?"

"Twenty-six."

He sighs. "Fuck. You had a job before? You got a degree or student loans and shit?"

I shake my head. "That's part of the problem. I didn't go to college. And Juniper's dad was my boss."

"So, he bought you off on a sexual harassment suit too? I'm sorry, Eden. I don't know if you loved this guy or what, but he sounds like a Grade A douchebag with a capital fucking D."

I lower my head and close my eyes. Did I love Nathan? My answer to that is so easy, but it makes me feel even shittier.

"I never loved him." I almost whisper it. "God, Vito." I tug my fingers through my hair. "Do you know what it's like to be so out of your depth? You probably don't. You have a great family. You're loved. You have people." I think back over the series of stupid decisions that brought me to LA, and maybe it's the fact that I'm in the back seat of the car and I can't look at Vito.

Maybe this is like some kind of confession or therapy session. Or maybe it's just the first time anyone has shown a real interest in what I've gone through, but I just start talking.

And once I start, I'm shocked how good it feels to let some of this go.

"What we had wasn't love," I say. "It was confusion. I was so lost in LA." I look out the window at the green lawns and mature trees, the clean streets and perfect sidewalks. Star Falls is literally a world away from where I'm from. "You've probably heard a little about my childhood from my aunt. My dad left me, and my mom died in prison. She was locked up for attacking a boyfriend with a hammer. And when Mom got sent away, her druggie boyfriend took responsibility for me."

Vito jerks the truck, but he quickly rights us. "Sorry," he growls. And it is a growl. "Did the boyfriend mistreat you?"

"No. Actually, Mom going away seemed to calm Bruce down a bit. He cleaned up his act and left me totally alone. I went to school, cooked for myself, cleaned the apartment. He got himself clean for a little while, but he definitely didn't want to be somebody's stepdad. He worked when he could and actually kept food in the house. Paid the bills." I bite my lip at the memory. Mac and cheese in a box isn't food to some people, but during the eighteen months Bruce lived with me, I never went to sleep hungry.

"That didn't last long," I continue. "Ma passed in prison. She had an appendicitis attack but didn't get medical attention fast enough. And then one day, when I was seventeen, Bruce packed up his shit while

I was at school. He left me a hundred dollars in cash and told me the rent was due on the first or I'd have to pay a penalty."

My eyes start to sting when I think about what happened next. How scared I was to be alone. "I'd gotten used to Bruce," I say quietly. "He wasn't family, but he didn't do anything bad. But as soon as he was gone, I needed to figure out how to pay the rent, how to buy groceries. That was when I decided to try to find my dad. Of course, that was impossible, but I did find my aunt, Shirley. She'd never stopped sending me birthday cards and letters over the years. When I told her Mom died and Bruce had left, Shirley came to my apartment. I begged her not to call child services. The last thing I wanted was to be put into foster care at seventeen."

Vito pulls into the parking lot of the hotel and turns off the car. He faces forward, his head lowered. "Go on," he urges.

"Well, the rest is pretty simple," I tell him. "Aunt Shirley paid the rent on my apartment until the day I turned eighteen. After that, I decided I wanted to move someplace that I picked. Someplace that I wanted to be. I had no idea what I wanted to do with my life. But I'd spent so much of my life living with people who didn't want me, in places I didn't want to be, I picked the most glamorous, exciting, fun place I could imagine. The City of Angels."

I smile even now, thinking of my former home. "I worked a ton of random jobs, lived in shitty apartments, and made a really bad choice dating a guy who showered me with attention but who wouldn't be there in the long run. But to answer your question, no. I'm kind of sorry to admit it. I got swept up in the romance of being wanted. But that's all it ever was until Junie. Because of her, I have zero regrets."

I smooth her sweaty curls back from her face and hope I've told him enough but not so much. I mean, I know my story is a lot, and there are still details I haven't shared. But he wanted to know my story and the situation, and that's it.

Most of it, at least. The bits I can share.

"Did you want to come in for a bit?" I ask him. "I think she should sleep for about another hour if I can get her inside without waking her up."

Vito is quiet, but he unfastens his belt and runs around to the rear doors to grab Junie's diaper bag.

I perform a feat of acrobatic wonder, sliding my hands under Junie's butt and setting her on my shoulder in such a smooth movement. She does wake up but then blinks those long lashes and mumbles, "Mama," and falls right back to sleep.

Vito locks the car, and I ask him to grab the keycard to my hotel room from a zipped pocket in the diaper bag. He unlocks the door and holds it open for me. I immediately go into the bedroom, where I have a pack and play set up for Junie. I tuck her in and wait to make sure she is going to stay asleep, then I quietly close the door behind me and head back to the living room.

I half expect to see Vito awkwardly standing by the door, just waiting to bolt after the miserable story I shared in the car. Instead, he's sitting on the couch, and he's spread out all the glossy listing sheets from each house we saw on the coffee table. He's looking over each one, but when I come back into the room, he stands.

"So, I sorted these in price order," he says, pointing to the sheets. "Maybe we go through each one and make a list of pros and cons. A couple of them I'd scratch off the list completely, but I want to know which ones you liked because if I saw red flags in a place you're thinking of buying, I got a buddy who can do a real home inspection for you. Figure out the cost to fix the problem, maybe get some money off the asking price so you can make the repair before you move in."

I'm staring at him, not saying a word, just taking

in everything he's saying. I realize I'm staring when he comes around the table with a concerned look on his face. "Are you okay? Am I being too pushy? If you want to make this decision on your own, I'll butt the fuck out, I just…"

I shake my head. "It's not that. I expected you to run after I told you all that shit about Junie's father. About my upbringing."

Vito cocks his chin and lifts one of those perfect, deep brown brows at me. He steps closer, and I can smell the same sensual aroma of his cologne.

"Eden." His voice is low as he reaches for my chin. He cups it in his hand, and his lips curl into a grin. "What you told me only makes me believe even more strongly that you're a fucking amazing woman. From everything I've seen, you're a totally dedicated and loving mom. You've had a hard life, and you're here for your fresh start. Why would I run from the strongest, sexiest, most resilient woman I've ever met?"

He releases my chin and chuckles. "Just don't tell Gracie I said that." He jerks a thumb toward the couch. "Come on, you got a house to buy and a home to make for yourself and that little girl."

He plops down onto the couch like this is something we've done a million times. I pull a pen and some paper from the hotel kitchenette and start making notes about the homes.

"While we're on the subject of this house, are you sure you want to buy?" he asks. "You're thinking you're going to stay in Star Falls?"

I nod. "Aunt Shirley's been after me to move here since my mom died." I toe off my shoes and shrug out of my wrap. It's getting warm in the late afternoon sun, but the windows in this all-suite extended-stay hotel don't open. If I want to cool off, I have to click on the air or lose a layer. "I figure if I buy a house now, I'll have enough equity by the time Juniper is grown to either sell if I need to or pull money out of the house. That's one thing I really want to do with my life," I say, admitting what I want more than anything.

"I never grew up in a house. Never had a savings account. Never knew how to manage money because there was literally never a spare penny. I want to have the life I always wanted. Of course, for my daughter, but not just for her. I want something good that we can share. I want more than what I've had."

As soon as I say the words, I remember that Vito's ex-wife left him because she wanted the finer things in life.

I hope he doesn't think I mean that. I don't know

what she wanted, and I sure don't want to judge a woman I don't know.

I don't think having some stability in my life and making sure I don't screw up the chance I've been given to make a normal life for my daughter is hard to understand.

But the smile he gives me washes away all my worries like a sudden storm on a sunny day. "You're going to do it," he says. "I can feel it. I got a good sense about you, Eden. You're a smart cookie."

I point to the listing sheet and think back to Robert's house. "Smart enough to make this work?"

"Is that the one?" he asks. His voice is low, and I'm suddenly aware of his knee gently touching mine.

I don't move away. "Yeah," I say. "I feel like it is." I look into his eyes. "I just hope I'm putting my trust in the right things this time."

"Things?" He scoots closer to me, until he's so close I feel the heat radiating from his arm beside mine. "Things are going to break, Eden. Dishwashers and roofs and sinks."

My heart starts hammering in my chest, and my palm gets sweaty. "I'm talking about the stuff that's harder to fix once it's broken."

His fingertips push my hair away from my neck, and he leans down to murmur against my ear.

"Hearts," he guesses. "Broken hearts can be fixed too."

All I can focus on is the pressure of Vito's thigh alongside mine and his sweet, light breath as he whispers against my skin.

"I'm a trained professional, you know. First aid, basic lifesaving. If you're going to put your trust in anyone, it might as well be me."

I shift a little and lift my face so our noses nearly touch. "I'm sure you've stopped plenty of hearts too," I say with a grin.

He snakes a hand behind my neck and slides his fingers into my hair. "You've got my heart and some other parts of me going haywire right now."

He tightens his fingers lightly, the slight tug on my roots sending a wave of arousal from my head all the way to my toes. I close my eyes and shiver, feeling the tiny hairs on my arms stand at attention. "Vito," I breathe.

"Yeah, babe?"

"Remember when you gave me permission to kiss you?"

"Uh-huh." He growls a laugh. "You've got an open invitation with me. You want it, you take it."

"Oh, thank God," I say, then I turn to him, lift one thigh, and straddle his lap.

CHAPTER 9
VITO

THE MINUTE EDEN settles into my lap, I slide my fingers under her hair, grip her neck, and pull her close.

I kiss her lightly at first, tasting her lips and getting used to the soft feel of her cheeks against my stubble.

Unlike when she kissed me in the car, she's not shy now. She closes her eyes and opens her mouth, nibbling my lips and panting sweet breaths against my mouth.

She opens her lips and flicks her tongue against mine, and that's when I know I'm fucked. A goner.

Her tongue dances against mine, and I swear I see sparks behind my eyes. A feral groan slips out of me. As if my arousal gives her permission to give in to hers, she laces her fingers behind my neck to pull me even closer.

She wiggles her hips against my lap, the denim of my jeans providing so much friction, I'm starting to get uncomfortably hard.

I pull my head back to catch my breath. Her cheeks are flushed, and her lips look swollen and bright red. I lower my face to her neck and nibble kisses along the sharp corner of her jaw.

She tips back, but I tighten my arms around her back and pull her toward me. I want to pick her up and lay her on this couch and do unspeakably dirty things to her, but I'm getting way too close to the point of no return.

She's sweet, she's smart, and she's seen some shit. She's got plans and priorities, and if her thick curves didn't have me hooked, everything else I'm learning about her would seal the deal.

"You're fucking hot, and you're all mine," I say.

"All yours?" she echoes.

I don't care if calling her mine is too much, too soon. She's mine right now. I'm not about to let anything come between us. Definitely not memories of my stripper ex who has no business fucking up our good time.

"At least for this afternoon," I say.

She slips off my lap to sit beside me. I throw an arm over her shoulder and lift her face to meet my eyes.

She grins and, twisting at the waist, grabs my face with both hands. "Yes," she whispers, then runs her nose along the stubble on my jawline.

She moans deep in her throat, and before I can stop it, my hand slides from her hip to her belly. She arches her chest against mine, and even though we are in the world's most awkward position, I feel her full breasts press against me.

I'm trying to figure out how we can get more comfortable while making an even more inappropriate scene on her couch when Eden shoves my chest lightly.

"Lie back a bit," she says, her voice thick and low.

I lean back, and she straddles my hips, but this time, she braces her hands on the back of the couch behind me so we won't tip off the front. She flicks her tongue along my lower lip while tugging the front of her V-neck top down a bit.

I take that as my invitation, and I cup her generous tits in my hands.

A whimper in her throat sends my dick into overdrive. She grinds her hips against mine, and we ravish each other's mouths while I hold her breasts, and she claws the couch behind my shoulders.

"I really want to kiss you here." I grunt the words against her lips, tightening my hold on her breasts.

She doesn't respond, just releases the couch and holds her arms in the air. I grab the hem of her tee and tug it up to reveal her belly. She bends her arms and works them through the sleeves, then sets the shirt beside us on the couch. She's wearing a dusty-pink-colored bra, the cups so thin I can see the sharp outlines of her hard nipples through the lace.

"Jesus fuck, babe," I pant. I swallow and just stare at her, taking in her body. "You are fucking unbelievable."

She looks down at her belly, pointing with a finger. "I've got a few stretch marks. Here…" She uses a finger to work a large circle, motioning over her abdomen. Then she lifts her hands to her breasts. "Here too," she whispers, her voice thick. "No one has seen all this since I had Junie."

"Really?"

I know her kid's only like a year old, but the fact that I'm the first—the only guy to experience this version of her body—gets me.

"Babe," I hiss, thumbing one nipple through the pink lace. "Everything about your body is fucking perfect."

We look into each other's eyes as I shove the fabric away to reveal her hard, copper-colored nipple.

I thumb the peak gently and suck air as she gasps and slams her eyes closed. "Sensitive?" I ask.

"Fuck yes," she breathes. "Don't stop."

I watch her lips part and her hips shimmy as I tweak both nipples between my fingertips. She throws her shoulders back and gasps, leaning into my hands and urging me to work her nipples harder.

"So good," she sighs, opening her eyes slowly. "Vito…"

I lower my face and suck her whole right nipple into my mouth. I hold the weight of her breast in my hand and swirl my tongue over the sensitive skin.

She gasps again and throws her head back, but my eyes are closed.

I'm focused on the pressure she's putting on my erection, the taste of her sweet flesh under my tongue, and the greedy noises that let me know she likes what I'm doing.

Suddenly, I hear a small, muffled song coming from the direction of Eden's bedroom. Juniper's awake. She's not screaming or crying. She's literally singing, "Maaaamaaaa."

"Fuck." I lift my mouth from her nipple and grin. "I'd almost be pissed if she weren't so damn cute."

Eden's grin is even bigger than mine. "Cutest little cockblock in Star Falls." She sighs and leans back to smooth the cups of her bra back into place. "I am so sorry," she says.

I shake my head and rub my face hard. "No apologies needed." I stand while she puts her shirt back on and adjust my cock in my jeans, praying it will go down quickly. "You need me to go?" I ask.

She pulls me close for a hug. We're nearly the same height, so when we're nose to nose, I can plant another kiss on her lips. "No," she whispers against my mouth. "Not until we've gone through the lists of pros and cons."

I slip my hands into the back pockets of her jeans and give her ass a playful squeeze. "One condition," I say. "We pick up where we left off sometime soon."

"Like, very soon," she promises.

She pulls away from me about as reluctantly as I let her go. She smiles at me, her hair mussed and her cheeks flushed as she heads to the bedroom.

"Look who's awake," she says to Juniper.

The hotel suite is starting to get dark, so I keep myself busy while Eden gets Juniper up by turning on the lights and grabbing a glass of water. I hear Eden call out that she's changing a diaper and will be right out, so I pour her a glass of water too and then go back to the listing sheets.

Eden and I spend the next couple of hours playing with Juniper and talking through the list of houses we looked at. There is a clear winner in both of our minds, and of course, it is the very first house we saw.

"So, you think you're going to make an offer?" I ask. I'm putting all the listing sheets into a stack while Juniper smashes a plastic cooking pot against the coffee table. I raise my voice a bit to call over the racket. "No more looking?"

Eden's in the kitchenette prepping some dinner for Juniper. "No," she says, meeting my eyes across the suite. "I think I'm going to trust my gut this time."

I've never been a man to believe in things like *the one* before, but I do believe in trusting my gut. And right now, my gut's telling me if there was ever a *one* for me, I've just found her.

———

Three weeks later, it's done.

Eden made an offer on the house, Robert accepted it, and the house passed all the inspections with flying colors.

Eden got approved for the mortgage, and since she was anxious to get out of the hotel, she was able to negotiate for a quick closing.

During that time, work was intense.

We had not one, but two unusually serious structure fires. For a small department like ours, one serious fire per quarter is not uncommon, but two in under a month put a strain on the team. Our captain suffered a twisted ankle at the first fire, so there was some shuffling of schedules while the cap healed up.

Eden and I didn't manage to fit in a proper date night, but we've had plenty of dates in, if you call dinner and heavy make-out sessions on the shitty hotel couch dates. By the time the week of the closing rolled around, Ma's friends were taking charge like a well-oiled machine.

"Vito, are you up yet?"

I hear Ma's voice and a noise like she's banging on my door with the heel of a stiletto shoe.

"Ma, fuck." It's not even eight in the morning if my phone's to be believed. Way too early for this shit. "What is it?"

"Can I come in?"

"Ma." I toss aside the covers and stride to the door in my pajama pants. There's a reason I don't sleep naked anymore, and her name is Lucia Bianchi.

I throw open the bedroom door and see the abominable noisemaker Ma was banging against my door. An industrial-sized tape roller that's as big as my mom's head.

"Where the hell did you get this, and why are you banging it on my door?"

Despite the early hour, Ma's fully dressed and made up to the nines. I grab her hand and stare at the glittery-looking hearts attached to her fingertips. "Did you get your nails done this early?"

Ma yanks her hand back and fake slaps me with it. "I got these done two days ago, Vito. I swear I could have little penises put onto my nails, and it would take you and your father a week to notice."

I blast a laugh through my lips and smooth my hair back. "I think Pops would notice dicks on your hands, Ma, but thanks for the visual. I just got a preview of my future nightmares."

I turn from Ma and grab a T-shirt from the floor. Ma shakes her head and snorts.

"Son, what did I tell you about leaving clothes on the floor? Are you going to do that at Eden's house?"

My jaw falls open, and I turn to stare at my mother. "Uh, excuse me?"

My mother rolls her eyes. "Oh please. It's not like we haven't noticed you've been gone a lot. Smiling all the time. And somehow, you seem to always leave the house right before Eden comes over for ladies' brunch. You tell me what all that means. Am I wrong? Are you or are you not seeing her?"

I shake my head and try not to smile. "You and your friends, Ma. You got to stop playing Sherlock Holmes with other people's lives. I thought you agreed to butt out of your kids' love lives after Franco and Chloe?"

Ma's face pinches, and she looks hurt. "Now that's not fair. Chloe and Franco are perfect together. That might not even have happened if I hadn't made sure your brother met the new girl in town. Now, honey, I'm not judging. I just…"

"Ma." I hold a hand up. "You did not wake me up on my day off to quiz me about my love life, did you? What's the tape for? You going to tape me to a chair until I confess I'm dating Eden?"

"You are." My mom looks so happy at that, all I can do is roll my eyes. "Son, ever since Michelle…"

"Don't finish that sentence." This time, my voice has a warning edge to it. Before I can say anything more, Pops comes up the stairs and makes his way down the hallway.

"Son, you're up? I told your mother I was going to head out. I didn't think you'd be vertical this early."

I yawn and shake my head. "I wasn't." My mother opens her mouth to complain, but I hold up a hand. "I'm up now. Where you off to, Pops?"

Mario Bianchi is dressed, showered, and shaved. He's shoved his glasses up on his head, and the silver hair that looks exactly like mine will in about thirty years is perfectly styled. He takes the tape roller from my mom's hand like it's a loaded weapon and shakes his head.

"Your mother's friends are taking Eden's move very seriously. I'm on box duty. Lucia is sending me out to the grocery stores to see if I can get some free cardboard boxes so Eden doesn't have to pay for them."

I shake my head and try not to laugh. "Ma, did you ask Eden about any of this? You realize she'd hardly unpacked when she had to move out of her rental. Most of her stuff is still in the moving boxes they came in from LA."

My mother gives me the most shit-eating grin and

crosses her arms over her chest now that her hands are free. "How would you know that?"

I roll my eyes like I'm fifteen again. "I was on the engine that responded the night of the house fire, remember?"

I wave my hands at my parents, both of whom are now crowded into my childhood bedroom. "Okay, look out. Both of you. I need a cup of coffee and a shower. Then I'll run errands with Dad and pick up boxes, body bags, whatever your friends want."

My mother pads across my room and flags me down with those blood-red nails. I lean down, and she kisses my cheek. "Make it a quick shower, honey. The ladies will be here soon."

I snort and meet my dad's eyes, but he just shrugs. He's as whipped by my mother as he was the day they met back in high school. As she brushes past him, he cops a feel of her ass, and I shout, "Pops! It's too early for that shit."

But Pops just looks back at me and waggles his eyebrows, then follows my ma back downstairs, closing my door behind them. I grab a towel and head into the bathroom that I shared with my sister Gracie until she moved in with her husband, Ryder.

While I love the extra space, I have to admit, I

miss having my sister around all the time. Things are definitely different being the last kid living at home.

I turn the water to scalding and climb under the spray, grinning about the secret that Eden and I've got going. We agreed to keep the fact that we're seeing each other quiet for now.

Shit's new, and until she's settled in her house, it's not like we're *dating* dating. Dinners at her place or walks with Juniper on my days off aren't exactly hot dates. But it's been more fun than I expected getting to know them while she waits to move into her new place.

It's been nice being excited about something for a change.

The shit at work hasn't changed, and that shit won't change unless I do something about it. I know what I have to do, but I'm just not sure I'm willing to do what it takes.

A fucking college degree.

I wouldn't even know how to do that. Show up with a goddamn backpack? What if the classes I need to take are on days I have to work?

By the time I get off my shift, all I want to do is sleep, do laundry, and catch up with Eden.

If I'd had the energy to think about going back to school before, now, things are changing. I've never dated anyone with a kid, and I can see from just the last month that having a kid is a full-time job.

I don't know how the hell my sister still does tattoos, manages to keep a house clean, cooks, and does everything else that needs to be done with three.

I decide to ask my pops about that when we're alone.

"You ready, son?"

Pops is twisting the lid on a travel mug of coffee when I clomp down the stairs.

"If that's for me, I am." I reach out my hand for the coffee, and Pops nods. "Thank you."

Ma is sitting at the dining room table, a bunch of lists and paperwork spread out. She's taking this move more seriously than Eden is, but I don't say a word. I kiss the top of her hair and realize that Ma's whole life has been about her kids and the people she loves.

She never went to college, never worked outside the home. All the energy and intelligence she has, she gives away. Whether she's volunteering at the animal shelter, babysitting her grandkids, or pounding on my door at an ungodly early hour of the morning, Lucia Bianchi is a force to be reckoned with. Glittery nails and all.

I wrap the arm that's not holding the coffee

around her neck and bend down toward her ear. "You're a fucking angel, you know that?"

Ma looks up at me in surprise, her pretty eyes heavy with mascara and liner. My words seem to hit her, and I can see every emotion cross her face. "Vito, language." She playfully swats at me, then blows a kiss at my father. "Don't dillydally," she reminds us.

"Oh, I'm going to dilly, baby." Pops is putting on a pair of work boots by the front door. "But I promise not to let V dally."

He grabs his keys, and I slide my feet into my running shoes and follow Pops out the front door. His truck's parked in the driveway, which means he probably cleaned it and gassed up even earlier this morning. Even though he's retired, he still gets up early, takes care of his truck like it's one of his kids, and never, ever complains, no matter what wild-goose chase Ma sends him on.

I buckle in and drink the scalding-hot coffee with cream and sugar, just the way I like it. "This is good, Pops. Thanks."

My dad nods, but I'm feeling shit today, so I got to say something more.

"How do you know exactly how I like my coffee?" I ask.

Pops shrugs. "Son, don't take this the wrong way,

but you've been living under my roof long enough, I'd have to be a dead man not to pick up on some of your habits."

He cracks himself up and I grin, but then he grows serious. "You know how I take my coffee," he reasons. "It's what families do. We pay attention to the small shit."

That gets me thinking.

I didn't notice Ma's new nails. Maybe it's because she's my mother, or maybe it's because she gets her nails done so often I can't keep up. Maybe I take a lot of things for granted. That question's got me feeling hot and uncomfortable.

"Was it hard?" I ask, swallowing a perfect sip of coffee. "Raising four of us? Ma always made it look so easy."

Pops chuckles. "I'm glad you think she did," he says. "But hell yeah, it was hard. But worth every second of the work. And that's what it is, kiddo. Work. But it's the best job on the planet if you've got people you love to do it with."

"What about work? Did Ma ever think about working outside the home? I never felt like we were struggling for money, but raising four kids… That shit ain't cheap."

Pops nods. "I could have moved up into management if I'd just had that stupid piece of paper." He shrugs. "I could have gone to school at night, but your mother and I decided I'd rather make less and be around more." He takes his eyes off the road for a split second to meet my eyes. "I sometimes worry we should have pushed you kids harder on the college thing. I always assumed my kids would go, but I was no help in that department."

"You did more than enough," I tell him, and it's true.

My parents cooked, kept a safe home, and never once let us worry about things that we had no business worrying about.

I grew up totally unlike Eden did, and while I've always appreciated my family and my upbringing, I'm starting to think I never really got how much having these two people as my parents made my life what it is.

It's a life I love, and no matter how lost I feel at times, with Mario and Lucia behind me, my siblings beside me, I can look to the future and know I can handle whatever I set my mind to.

I just have to make up my mind.

"So, Pops," I say, "what do you think about stopping for breakfast after we get Ma's boxes? My treat."

My dad shoots me a look. "Double bacon breakfast sandwiches, and you got a deal."

I lean back in the passenger seat and finish off the coffee my pops made. "You got a deal."

Some decisions in my life have been hard, but I think one just got a lot easier.

CHAPTER 10
EDEN

"EDEN?"

I bounce Juniper on my knee and look up at the woman who's just called my name. "Hi," I call out, waving my hand so she knows who I am. I secure the diaper bag over my shoulder and follow the nicely dressed woman into an incredibly small office.

"Have a seat," she says, motioning to the chairs on the opposite side of her desk.

"I hope you don't mind I brought my daughter," I say, stating the obvious. "I wasn't able to line up childcare, but that's part of what I'm hoping to learn about today. If doing this is realistic for a single parent."

"Absolutely. Not a problem at all." The woman reaches over her desk to shake my hand. "I'm

Catherine Jones, and I'm an admissions counselor. I can answer any questions you have about the programs we offer, tuition costs, things like that. If I need to refer you to one of my colleagues in student life or financial aid, we can probably get everything you need before you leave today."

"Oh, okay. Great. Thank you." I shake her hand and sit down, giving Juniper a teething toy shaped like a little banana with soft plastic bristles at one end. She jams it in her mouth and chews contentedly on my lap.

"My nieces had one of those." Catherine points at the banana. "So cute." She's pulling up a file on her computer while she talks. "Your application materials are complete, and everything looks good. What specific questions can I answer for you today?"

I bite my lower lip and think through the laundry list of worries I have. I start with the easiest question first. "You saw my high school transcripts. I'm a little worried about how much time I'll need to spend on general education requirements before I can apply to a four-year college."

Catherine nods. "Very understandable. You were interested in finance?"

I nod. "I think so. I know I want to learn about money—accounting, bookkeeping, and investments."

"That's what makes the community college model so effective." She goes on to explain that this community college offers a lot of free webinars in different disciplines so that enrolled students can learn a bit about each field of study and the careers that students can pursue.

"We also offer some of our upper-level courses online. Most of the foundations are still offered in person, but you might be able to take up to half the classes you need online from home."

"And if I want to get a degree from a four-year college or university later, those online classes transfer?"

She nods. "Most advisers will help you plan out a curriculum so that you can successfully transfer most if not all of the credits you earn here." She tells me about two colleges in the area that offer transfer incentives to students who have earned associate degrees from area community colleges.

"You know what I might recommend for you?" she says, cocking her head. "Sit in on a class as a guest. We have a new instructor, and she's fantastic. While I can't make any promises, she might be willing to talk with you after class a bit about jobs and her career path." She gives Junie a grin. "You would need to line up a babysitter for that, though."

I nod. "How soon do you think I could sit in?" The back of my SUV is loaded with empty boxes, thanks to Lucia and her friends getting me ready to move. If all goes as planned, I'll be closing on my brand-new house tomorrow. That means weeks of unpacking and getting settled.

I'd like to visit a class as soon as possible so I can spend the coming month thinking about the next big decision—not just where I want to set down roots for my future, but what I want to be when I grow up. And whether getting a degree and going back to school may be part of that plan.

Catherine is tapping away at her keyboard. "Hmm," she says. "Well, this is short notice, but the class I had in mind for you meets tonight on campus at seven and is three hours long. You don't have to stay for the whole class, but if you do, you might catch a few minutes with the instructor." She continues tapping and changing screens. "We have a class taught by a different instructor that might be good for you as well, and that one is tomorrow at noon."

I can't do that one. I know that for sure. I'm supposed to do the final walk-through on the house tomorrow at noon. I've already lined up my aunt Shirley to watch Junie until she has to head into work at three. I can't very well ask her to come over tonight too.

I worry my lip between my teeth. There is someone else who might be willing to watch Juniper. Someone whom I trust with my daughter completely. But this is a big ask. A very big ask.

Then something occurs to me. "Catherine," I say, "do you think I can leave class early without insulting the instructor? I might be able to get a babysitter on short notice, but not for the whole evening."

Catherine smiles. "I'm sure that won't be a problem. Why don't you arrive a few minutes early and see if you can mention it? Then just sit toward the back of the class and slip out quietly. Most three-hour classes break midway through anyway."

"Okay, one second." I grab my phone and stare at it. Vito and I have only known each other about six weeks. Is it way too soon to ask for this kind of help? I don't know, but it's better to find out sooner rather than later how he feels about things like this.

Me: Is there any chance I could ask you for a huge favor tonight? If you can spare an hour or two to help me with Junie, I promise I will pay you back any way you'd like...

I add some kissy lips emojis, hit send, and then type out one more text.

Me: But seriously, if tonight's not good, it's okay. I can make other…

Before I even finish typing the message, I have a reply. Two thumbs-up emojis.

Vito: Where and when, babe? Just tell me where to be.

My heart flips over in my chest. He didn't ask questions, didn't hesitate.

Something breaks open inside me, and suddenly, I'm feeling excited. Confident, even. Maybe all of this is truly the life I was meant to have.

Supportive people.

A man who cares enough about me to show up without asking questions. Not a man who shows up armed with a team of lawyers and confidentiality agreements.

I look at Catherine and let the first real ray of hope I've felt since I moved to Star Falls brighten my smile. "I have childcare," I say. "What do I need to do?"

"Oh, wonderful." She taps a message into her computer and then prints off a form for me. "I've alerted the instructor through our messaging portal, but take this to class."

I take the form and tuck it into my diaper bag then tap out a message to Vito.

Me: Meet me at my place around 6:15? I can't wait to pay you back for this.

I add a whole line of kiss emojis, and I toss in a couple of eggplants and peaches just for fun. Then I thank Catherine, double-check I have the form I need for tonight, and head to my car with a stupid grin on my face.

Who'd have imagined when I packed up and moved away from the noise and hustle of LA that my dreams weren't where I always thought they were?

If you'd told me four years ago that taking a community college class would get me feeling so hopeful, I would have laughed. But now, I'm about to have the home of my dreams and a plan for a possible career. And that's got me feeling giddy.

The life I've always wanted has never been closer.

"I fed her dinner and changed her diaper." Vito is holding Junie in his arms, following me through the maze of boxes in my hotel room. "If she cries or drools a lot, try a teething ring from the freezer first."

I am moving at warp speed through the instructions, but as the minutes tick away, I'm feeling less and less confident in this plan.

All the excitement of the afternoon comes crashing down as I realize that just because Vito may be willing to do this doesn't mean I'm ready.

"Teething ring first," he repeats, a small smile on his face.

He looks more gorgeous than ever, wearing a soft gray T-shirt under a well-broken-in blue flannel shirt. He's got on distressed dark blue jeans and running shoes, and he smells so good, I seriously rethink my whole plan.

"You know what?" I say, backpedaling so fast I'm feeling dizzy. "This was too much. I'm closing on the house tomorrow, and Junie is teething. I'm not going to go."

Vito slides a hand along my hip and gives me a reassuring squeeze. "First of all, I am trained in life-saving procedures," he says. "Your daughter will be safe with me. But you still haven't told me what's got you so frazzled. Where are you going? Why do you seem more terrified to leave me alone with your daughter than you did to put in an offer on a house? I've been alone with kids, Eden."

"Oh no. It's not that. I trust you completely." I'd told Vito what time to come by, but I haven't yet explained where I am going and why. "I'm feeling super insecure about this all of a sudden. It's stupid. I was excited all day, but now that it's, like, real…" I sigh.

He sets Juniper down on her playmat and makes sure she grabs a toy before pulling me close. "Babe," he says, his voice low against my ear. "Whatever this is, I'm here for it. Babysitting, moral support."

I peek over at Junie, who is calmly playing by herself. I loop my arms around Vito's waist and rest my head against his chest. "I feel so stupid. So much is changing so fast. We've been living out of boxes forever, Vito. I'm tired. I'm confused."

He holds me firmly, and I let the warmth of his muscled chest support my weight. I duck my chin and hide my face in the spicy cologne that clings to his shirt.

"You wanted me here for something. Whatever it was mattered. If you don't want to share it, you don't have to. But why don't you try to go and just see if you feel better. Sometimes the hardest part is getting out the door. Once you're in the car, you aim for the destination, and don't stop until you get there. I'll be right here with Junie when you get back."

I'm suddenly struck by an idea. It seems foolish, but I'm blurting it out before I can talk myself out of it. "Come with me?" I ask. "I've been looking into taking some classes at the community college. I got a guest pass to sit in on a class tonight. I'm not going to stay the whole time. I'll leave as soon as there's a break—or sooner, if it goes too long. I can't bring Junie into class, but maybe we could bring the stroller and you could walk the campus until I'm done?" I lift my face and look into his gorgeous eyes. There's a thick dusting of stubble on his chin, which he'll shave before he goes back on shift Saturday. I reach a hand to stroke the roughness.

He takes my fingers and brings them to his lips. "I'm not normally one for signs and shit," he says, "but I've been thinking about checking out the community college myself. Been talking myself out of it for months now. This might just be the sign I need to give school a little more thought."

I hold his face with both my hands. "Are you serious? You've been thinking about going back to school?"

He chuckles. "I wouldn't say go back. I haven't spent one second of my life on a college campus." He slides his hands under my hair and sighs. "Not having a degree has held me back in the department. I've been passed over for countless promotions. The last two were just a few months ago," he admits. "It might get me feeling inspired, being on a college campus. You never know. Maybe I'll look around and be like, yeah, this shit's not for me. Either way, I'm down to go, Eden. You got the stroller?"

I nod. "It's in the back seat of the SUV. I took it out of the trunk to make room for all the boxes."

"All right. Do we need to pack anything, or is she good to go?"

He's still holding me, and I feel a strange sense of relief flood my chest. "Vito," I say. I pull back from him and look into his beautiful eyes. "Are you sure about this? Maybe it's all too much, too soon. I'm about to move into a house, and I'm..."

He leans forward and plants a kiss on my lips, a light, teasing one with a gentle sweep of his tongue against mine.

"Eden," he says, "too soon for what? What's too much?" He swallows and looks like he's measuring his words. "I'm in this, babe. Not, like, move into your new house with you in this, but I care about you. I'm falling for you. I'd spend time with you if all you wanted to do was sit on the couch and watch kid shows for hours. Doing something like this? Something that might bring you closer to your dreams?"

He kisses me again. "I respect what you're trying to do with your life. If the only way I can support you is by kicking you in the pants when you're doubting yourself, then I hope your fine behind is ready to meet my toes."

I shake my head, laughing in spite of the tears of gratitude that sting my eyes. "Okay, okay," I say. "I just hope you still feel that way in six months when I've got a leaky sink and a mountain of homework."

He releases me and holds up a finger. "Leaky sink, I got. Homework's all you." He chuckles.

We gather up Junie and head over to the campus. We find the visitor parking lot, and I fish a notebook and the pass that Catherine from Admissions gave me out of the diaper bag.

Vito sets up the stroller and puts Junie in, then fastens the little safety straps. She kicks and laughs, then immediately tosses a toy onto the sidewalk.

Vito picks it up and pretends to kiss the bunny's ears. "It's all right, bunny. Just a scratch." Junie's squealing for it, and he hands it back to her but then motions toward me. "Go on," he says. "We'll be fine. If you have any trouble finding us when you're done, just look for the guy doing wheelies with a stroller."

I shake my head but grab his arm. "Walk me to class?"

A sexy grin spreads across his face. "Lead the way." As we follow the campus map to the building where the math and finance classes are held, Vito lowers his voice. "I like the idea of you being a sexy schoolgirl," he says. "Maybe we can act that out sometime."

Heat pools in my belly, and I rub his back, letting my hand graze his incredibly fine ass. The fall sun is setting and even if anyone saw me grab his behind, I don't think they'd care. The campus looks pretty quiet at this hour, commuter students doing exactly what we are, hustling between the parking lot and night classes.

There are some students hanging around in groups, though. Kids carrying enormous backpacks, talking, laughing. Some running with headphones on. I don't see any babies or children, not that I expected to.

There could be plenty of people enrolled who left their kids at home with sitters or spouses. I'm fortunate to have Junie with me. And to have someone by my side to keep an eye on her while I stick a toe in this scary new pond.

"So, what's the class?" Vito steers the stroller, expertly avoiding a crack in the pavement before we reach the nicely maintained path that leads toward the instructional center.

"It's just an intro course," I explain. "Personal

Accounting. I think it covers the basics of money management and bookkeeping."

He nods. "Love it for you. You lost me at accounting."

I slip my hand into the back pocket of his jeans and squeeze. "You know they have all kinds of programs here. Have you ever thought about what kinds of classes you'd take if you wanted to go back for a degree?"

He shakes his head. "And therein lies my problem. I'd probably end up spending more time on the shit that was fun than what I needed to do to actually get a degree."

As we approach the building, I hang back with the stroller. "I won't be long," I tell him. "I'll let the instructor know that I can't stay the whole time. I'll slip out in an hour—or even sooner if it's really boring."

I hold the door open for a couple kids rushing by, but Vito shakes his head. "You stay as long as you want. We'll go exploring."

I clutch the entry pass in my suddenly sweating hand. I hear the buzz of shoes hitting the tile floors, the squeak of the stroller wheeling along beside me.

This is really happening. I've never set foot in a college classroom, and I feel like an impostor. My stomach flips over, and I'm glad I skipped dinner, just eating a banana while I fed Junie her dinner.

"Hey." I hear his voice against my hair. "This you?" He nods toward a closed classroom door. The lights are off, but we're early. Class doesn't start until seven, and it's quarter till.

I nod. "Looks like this isn't a class people come early to. Maybe it sucks?"

He lifts my chin in his hand and kisses me lightly. "Maybe it will. You'll find out," he says lightly.

"Excuse me." A really, really young-looking guy carrying a massive backpack steps around the stroller and yanks open the classroom door. He turns on the light and props the door open. For a minute, I think he might be the instructor, but he takes a seat and plugs in a laptop, so I think maybe he's just a student arriving early.

Vito wheels the stroller out of the path of the door. "You going in?" he asks.

"Yeah." I worry my lower lip between my teeth.

"Maaamaaa." Junie tosses her bunny to the floor, so I release Vito's hand to bend over and get it.

"Juniebug, Mama's going to go into that room right there, and you're going to go for a walk with Vito. Does that sound like fun?" I kneel down to give her back the bunny and kiss her cheek when I hear the clacking of very high heels on the floor.

I hurry to stand, guessing that those are not the shoes of a student. I see an absolutely gorgeous, willowy woman with shoulder-length blond hair striding toward the classroom with a slim leather briefcase in one hand. She's wearing black eyeglasses, but her outfit screams money. She looks elegant, expensive, put together.

I see her look from the stroller to me to Vito, and I clutch the paper in my hand. I'm sure we look totally out of place, but the way she's looking at us makes me feel like maybe Catherine was wrong. Maybe this instructor doesn't allow visitors? She pulls the glasses from her face and cocks her head, and that's when I see Vito's body go stiff.

"Vito?"

The stunning woman knows his name. I look from her to him and back again.

He nods at the woman and releases a sigh so dramatic, I'm sure she hears it. "Wow. There you are. Nice to see you again, Michelle."

CHAPTER 11
VITO

WELL, if I'd thought Eden going to college was some kind of sign, I'll be good goddamned if this isn't my sign to run like hell in the opposite direction.

"Vito? Holy shit. Is that you?" Michelle, my ex-wife, glides up to us on heels so high, I can't help but think they are a step down from the stripper shoes she used to wear.

I'm not being petty, though.

I'm stunned and uncomfortable.

Of course, I'd heard she was in town, but running into her here?

No fucking way.

Michelle's brain's got to be running a million miles an hour. She looks from Eden to Juniper to me, and then her whole demeanor softens. "Well, this is a surprise. Can I give you a hug?"

I open my arms and let her give me a hug, but I don't really return the gesture.

As soon as she releases me, she sticks her hand out toward Eden. "I'm Michelle Davis. Vito and I are, uh, old friends."

Shit. This is going to get even weirder if I don't do something fast.

"Babe." I turn to Eden. "This is Michelle, my ex-wife."

I watch as Eden woodenly shakes Michelle's hand. "Hi," she says quietly.

"And is this…" Michelle gives Juniper a huge smile, and she bends down to look into the stroller. "Oh my God, you're adorable. Hi."

Michelle waves at Junie, and I realize it must look like this is my family. But I'm okay with that. I'm not sure how to feel.

Uncomfortable is a fucking given.

But then I remember why I'm here in the first place. I swallow back my feelings and motion toward the classroom door.

"What are you doing here?" I ask Michelle. "You teaching?"

She smiles and looks genuinely happy. "I am,"

she says. "I moved back to town to take care of my grandfather. You remember Granddad."

I nod, and she continues.

"I opened my own business, and I'm teaching here part time at night." She looks from Vito to me. "What are you doing here?"

I step closer to Eden and put my hand on her lower back. "Eden has a guest pass to sit in on your class." I realize I'm talking for her, and I'm sure that is the last thing she wants. Although when I look at her, Eden still looks shocked speechless. "Babe?" I nod at her.

That seems to break Eden out of her trance. She smiles self-consciously and offers Michelle the sheet of paper that she's nearly crumpled into a ball. "I was hoping to sit in on your class tonight. Catherine from Admissions emailed about me."

Michelle sets her briefcase on the floor and claps her hands. A couple more students have arrived, and they walk past us to get into the classroom. "Hey there," she says, greeting the students. "Go on in. I'll be right there. Hi Lacey, are you prepared for your presentation?"

One of the two women she talks to looks older than we are. She slaps her thigh and laughs loudly. "Ms. D, you know I'm ready for my A."

Michelle grins. "I'm happy to hear it. I'll be right in." She steps to the side and puts a hand on Eden's arm. "Catherine emailed me about you. I'm so glad you decided to visit. Do you have any questions before class starts? If you're able to stay late, I'm happy to chat with you after class too."

Eden looks from Michelle to me, then back again before answering. "No questions. Thank you. I was going to say that I have childcare for a little bit, but I might not stay the whole class. I didn't want to be rude and get up and leave in the middle."

My mind is spinning so fast, I can't think straight.

Michelle shakes her head and takes the pass from Eden. "That's no problem. You leave whenever you need to." She pulls a pen out from her briefcase and scribbles something on the back of the pass, then hands it back to Eden. "This is my work email and phone number. If you have any questions after class, you let me know. I can make an appointment and see you in my office." She looks at Juniper. "And if you need to bring your daughter, please do. I do a lot of work with female clients. I like to help women understand how to make money and how to manage it." She gives me a grin. "No offense to you, Vito."

"None taken," I say, my lips as tight as my gut.

Michelle is being really nice, and I shouldn't be

surprised. She's good people. She always was. But after all these years, why couldn't I have just run into her at a gas station or something?

Eden tucks Michelle's contact information into her notebook. "Thank you so much. That's really generous of you."

Michelle pulls the black glasses back over her face. "Not at all. This is literally what I do. Come on in." She looks back at me and Juniper. "V, there's a little playground over by the early childhood center. Your daughter might be able to get some time in the swings while you wait."

I nod stiffly and force a smile on my face. I won't correct her about Juniper. Unless Eden says something, I'm fine with Michelle thinking this is my family.

Eden turns to follow Michelle into the classroom, but then Michelle turns back to me with a stunning smile. "It was great seeing you, V."

I bristle at her familiar nickname. I grip the handles of the stroller, hoping I don't snap the plastic. "You too, Michelle." Then I look at Eden. "Stay as long as you want," I tell her.

Her face is pale and her lips tight, but she follows Michelle into the classroom without looking back.

It's only after the door is shut and I'm alone with

Juniper that I realize I should have kissed Eden goodbye.

"So, Juniper, that was freaking awkward." I talk to the little girl the whole walk.

She's surprisingly quiet after leaving her mom, but I'm hoping that she's seen enough of me over the last few weeks that the excitement of being someplace new and being out in the fresh air has her nicely distracted.

I peek over the stroller and make sure Junie is okay. She's tucked under a light blanket, kicking her legs and babbling.

What are the odds that my ex-wife is teaching the class Eden wanted to visit? My gut twists in a knot, and I realize I have to talk to someone, but then the bunny hurtles right out of the stroller.

"Hey," I call out, stepping on the brakes on the stroller. I kneel in front of Junie, a huge smile on my face. "Where is he?"

I tap the blanket on her lap, and she laughs and screeches.

I stand up and look all around and pretend I don't

see the bunny. "Is he…here?" I peek inside the sleeve of my flannel.

"Bunny!" Junie shouts, and she suddenly lifts her little hips up and out of the seat like she's going to get up and show me where the bunny is.

"Whoa there." The safety belt is on, so she can't get out, but I don't want her tipping out of the stroller the first time I'm alone with her. "No injuries, no tears," I point a finger at Junie. "I'll get that bunny, but you stay right here, okay? Is that him right there?"

I motion off into the grass, and Junie shouts "bunny" again. I grab it and hand it off to Juniper before we head toward the playground.

I'm expecting it to be locked, but I'm shocked to see that two other kids are playing, with an older lady sitting nearby on a bench looking at her phone.

A security guard in uniform wanders over and waves at me. The guy surprises me by calling my name. "Vito?"

As I get closer, I recognize him, and I reach out a hand and shake his. "Hey, man. You're Martinez, right?"

He nods. "Yeah. Nick Martinez." That's when it hits me. Nick used to be a waiter at my brother's restaurant.

"What've you been up to, man? No more Italian dinners?"

He shakes his head and pats his stomach. "I miss Benito's cooking. I loved that job, but I couldn't hack the hours. I'm enrolled in night school here, trying to get an associate's. It's tough out there without a degree. I'm doing security part-time and doing some training over at the gym."

"I hear that shit," I say. "Good to see you, man. You locking up the playground? We'll get out of your hair if it's closing time."

Nick shakes his head. "Nah, it's fine. If there are families here, I let them stay until class is out. I'll lock up when the classroom buildings close for the night." He looks at me and cocks his head. "I didn't know you had a family, Vito. Congrats, man."

"I wish I could take credit for her," I laugh. "This is Juniper, my uh...girlfriend's daughter." I jerk a thumb behind me even though the instructional center is quite a ways away. "My girl's visiting a class tonight. She's thinking of enrolling." I don't know if Eden considers herself my girlfriend, but I'm a guy alone with a kid who isn't mine, so saying anything else seems like asking for trouble.

If I'm honest, I'd be more than happy with that label for Eden.

Nick takes a few steps closer and then holds up a finger when there's a crackle at the radio on his chest. He reports in to dispatch with his location and then returns to our conversation. "All good," he says. "We had a teacher lose her phone and laptop, but she found it." He grins. "Exciting work when the case solves itself."

I chuckle, but since Nick doesn't seem like he's going anywhere in a hurry, I decide to ask the question on my mind. "Hey, you mind if I ask you how it is? Going to school when you're not, like, eighteen years old?"

Nick nods. "I got to be honest, I was scared shitless. I barely made it through high school. I passed, but I didn't care about learning. Had no clue what I wanted to do with my life." He shrugs. "This is an easy gig, but if I ever want to support a family, buy a house, I got to be okay with a little discomfort. You know?"

"Nah, I get it, man. You doing good now? Classes hard?"

Nick shakes his head. "It all depends on the teacher. Some are great. They really care about helping adult students succeed."

I extend a hand to him and clap him on the shoulder. "You ever want to grab a meal at Benito's, let me know. My treat."

Nick grabs my number and saves it in his phone. "I'll do that. You end up taking some classes, let me know. I'll give you a campus tour." He laughs and points to the playground. "Have fun, little lady. I'll come back after class to lock up."

Nick wanders off, answering yet another crackling call on his radio, so I wheel the stroller through the small fence and park it on the spongy rubberized ground that covers the play area.

"Do you want to go on the swing?" I kneel beside the stroller, and Juniper holds her arms out. But when I don't move fast enough, she starts scrambling out of the stroller.

I grab her hand and swoop her up with a happy shout. She giggles and settles into my arms, and together, we walk over to the baby swing.

She slides into the swing seat without a problem, and I start slowly, giving her a few small pushes.

She delights in the movement, kicking her legs and looking back at me. "Yeah." I cheer. "Is that fun, Junie? You like the swing?"

I have just given her another little push when my phone buzzes in my pocket. Thinking it might be Eden, I grab it and answer without checking who it is.

"How'd it go?"

"No clue what you're talking about, bro." My brother Franco sounds confused.

"Ah, dickhead, I expected somebody else. What's up?" I tuck the phone against my cheek and push Juniper with one hand.

"I thought I'd see if you want to grab a drink at Benito's. You're off tonight, right?"

"Yeah, but I'm babysitting. Eden had a thing, so I'm at a park with Juniper."

"Huh," Franco grunts. "You getting tied down finally?"

It's the word finally that has me shaking my head. "Fuck, man, you'll never guess who we ran into tonight."

I explain everything to Franco and leave nothing out.

"Well, that's freaking fucked up. Did Eden bail?" he asks.

I roll my eyes at the big brotherly support. "She went into class, so she didn't bail on school. Or do you mean bail on me?"

Franco is quiet for a minute, as if he just, for the first time, heard what he said and how it sounded. "Fuck, sorry. That's not what I meant. How did you feel seeing Michelle? Did she look as good as ever?"

I chuckle. "Yeah, of course. Michelle could wear a paper bag, and she'd be hot as hell."

"And?" Franco presses.

"And what?" Junie is twisting back to look at me, so I come to stand in front of the swing and pull her toward me with one hand while I hold my phone in the other.

"You think you want her back? How do you feel, V?"

I don't even have to think about how I feel. I know. "I don't want to go back. There's no doubt about that."

"What about Eden?" he asks. "You think you want to give the whole relationship thing a try again?"

Juniper's grin is enormous, her drooly lips parted to reveal her tiny baby teeth as she swings. "I'm in this. No question in my mind," I say, slowing the swing with one hand. "I don't know what Eden thinks, but for me, this is it. This is what I want."

Franco snorts, and I can just picture him shaking his head. "You going to be cool if she's taking classes with Michelle? I can't fucking believe your stripper ex-wife is teaching college."

"Hey, hey," I say, a warning in my voice. "Michelle was always smart. You know that. Big dreams, big goals. I wouldn't be surprised by anything she set her mind to doing." I do have to consider his question, though.

"About damn time," he says, and I can hear the smile in his voice. "Happy for you, bro. Can I give you two pieces of advice?"

"Sure," I say, but I probably don't want to hear whatever sage advice he's about to give.

"Make sure Eden knows how you feel. Offer to talk to Michelle if that would help. Don't let anything go unsaid, so you never have to question whether you did everything you could to make this work."

His words hit me deep. He knows I did damn near everything I could think of to make things work between Michelle and me, but it wasn't enough.

"What's the other thing?" I ask, pulling a fussy Juniper from the swing. "And make it quick. I got a toddler I got to chase." I set Junie on the rubbery turf and let her run to a seesaw thing that looks like a plastic horse.

"Don't tell Ma that Eden met Michelle. Keep that shit buttoned down."

I bark out a laugh. "Got it, Franco. Thanks for the call. Rain check on drinks." I hang up and slide the phone into my back pocket just in time to help Juniper climb onto the back of a yellow plastic horse.

I haven't been this close to dating someone seriously since Michelle and I broke up.

It may be awkward, but if this is what I want, I need to do everything I can to make it work.

And maybe, just maybe, this time, I'll be enough.

CHAPTER 12
EDEN

THIS IS GOING to be the longest three hours of my life.

Okay, no, scratch that. I'm being dramatic.

Going through labor and delivery alone... Those were the longest hours of my life.

But at least I had a gorgeous baby to snuggle at the end of the pain.

Sitting in a classroom being taught by the ex-wife of the guy I'm into? This was definitely not on the list of things I expected to live through in my life.

As soon as I realized that my instructor was Vito's ex-wife, time dragged. Of course, the first thing I fixated on was how goddamn gorgeous Michelle was.

For the most part, I'm comfortable with my body with its stretch marks and many flaws, but come on.

"All right, everybody." Michelle claps her hands together to silence the small talk and chatter right at the stroke of seven. "Thank you all for coming tonight. I know most of you have jobs, families, and a lot of responsibilities outside of this class, so even though this is our sixth week together, I want to thank you for showing up. This is also my not-so-subtle reminder to silence your phones and keep your attention—" she sweeps a hand toward the whiteboard affixed to the wall behind her "—on the work we're here to do."

She turns her back to us for a moment and writes a word on the whiteboard in blue marker. I watch her arms, thin and moving fast in a pristine white shirt, before she faces the classroom, adjusts the black-framed glasses over her eyes, and points to me.

"We have a visitor tonight, someone who is thinking of enrolling in this course. Eden," she says, giving me a warm smile that hits me right in the face like a spotlight. "While you are a guest, you're part of this class, so feel free to raise your hand and ask questions anytime."

I feel the eyes of half the class on me. My cheeks burn, but I manage to smile and mouth thank you, even though my throat is suddenly so dry, I don't think I could speak even if I wanted to.

I must look at the clock on the wall every ten seconds because it gives me something to look at other than Michelle's beautiful ass in that pencil skirt.

It's hard not to wonder how someone lifts themselves up from a job stripping to teaching in less than five years' time. If she could do it, maybe there is hope that I can overcome my circumstances too.

With a good babysitter and a plan, I could easily have a degree under my belt in five years.

Michelle dims the lights a bit and turns on a projector that's attached to her laptop. She's pulled up a financial statement and is talking through the different parts, what information appears, and what each thing means. It's like a puzzle the way she explains it, translating things like fixed assets and long-term liabilities with examples that actually make sense. She relates everything to real-world situations, and I'm so caught up, before I realize it, it's after eight and she's turning on the lights and motioning to the clock.

"Everyone, I'd like five extra minutes to talk with our visitor over the break. Enjoy your break."

Most of the students grab their phones but leave their backpacks on their desks. I'm kind of surprised they're just going to leave their stuff, but then again, this isn't LA. This is Star Falls, so maybe stealing backpacks isn't a problem on this campus?

I'm still in my chair when Michelle rushes up to me, a huge smile on her face.

She pulls the chair of the kid sitting next to me close and sits beside me. "So, Eden." She's literally beaming, and again, I cringe a little at how damned pretty she is. "I am so glad you stayed until the break. I wanted to make sure you didn't have any questions. What did you think of class? Is this what you expected?"

I nod, not sure what I expected. "It was really interesting," I say honestly. "Not confusing at all. To be honest, I didn't really know what to expect. I was trying to keep an open mind, but this was really interesting." I hesitate a second before saying what's on my mind because I don't want to seem like I'm sucking up to her, but then I just say it. "You're actually a really good teacher." I rush on awkwardly, worried I sound like I'm judging her. "Not that I didn't think you would be. I just mean if I'd had teachers like you in high school, I probably would have gone to college."

She nods, presses her lips together, and hums in agreement. "You know, that's exactly why I want to teach." She motions to the whiteboard. "Please don't take this the wrong way, but they pay us next to nothing to teach. I don't do it for the money. I didn't learn from my family how to manage money or build wealth. I learned by getting into debt and nearly killing myself to dig out of it. I want to help save as many people—and frankly, as many women—as I can from going down that path."

She's quiet then, as if expecting me to admit that I'm here to manage debt. I don't have any, but that's not because I learned how to do anything the right way.

I take a deep breath and admit just a little of what I feel safe sharing. "I have a small trust. A structured settlement. It won't last forever, so I'm hoping to learn how to be responsible with money so I can make good choices with the funds I have while they are coming in. And then, I'd like to find a career that I can enjoy once I'm able to work full time. I'm raising my daughter alone at the moment, her father isn't in the picture, and…"

And that's where things start to devolve in my brain. Vito, what he is to me, how long we've been dating… But Michelle reaches out and lightly touches my arm.

"Hey," she says gently. "I get it. And listen, about the elephant in the room. I'm so glad you came to class tonight. I'm sure if you've talked to V about me at all, you know I used to dance." She laughs and shakes her head as if stripping brings up fond memories. "I can't tell you how many clients I have now who six, seven years ago used to stuff singles in my thong." She covers her mouth and full-belly laughs. "Now they hand over their entire portfolio for me to manage." She shrugs like it's not a big deal. "An honest living is an honest living, and I'm not ashamed of my past career. You shouldn't apologize or be ashamed of your circumstances either."

She points up at the clock. "I need to hit the ladies' room before the break is over, but I'm serious. Vito and I were married, but that was a lifetime ago and this is a small town. I knew I'd run across him or one of the Bianchis eventually. I'm just so glad he has you and your daughter. Vito is..." She looks down at the desk, a brief look of sadness on her face. "A good man, through and through," she says. "No matter what happened between us, I, for one, have zero hard feelings."

I gather my things and stand with her. "I'm sorry I can't stay for the whole class," I say. "It's already past my daughter's bedtime."

"No problem. You go ahead." She pushes back her chair and gives me a dazzling smile. "You have my cell and my email. Make an appointment anytime you want some informal advice or guidance. Or if you need help managing the trust you have. This isn't a sales pitch. I'm happy to help you if I can. Give my best to Vito."

She gives me a wave and then heads into the hallway, her high heels clicking until I can't hear them anymore.

I grab my phone and punch in a text to Vito.

Me: I'm ready. Meet me out front of the building?

Then I gather my things and head outside into the cool, dark evening. I need a few minutes to compose my thoughts.

Butterflies of stress flap a thousand little wings in my belly, and my phone buzzes with a response from Vito.

Vito: I can't wait to hear everything. We'll be right there.

Just seeing his words makes me realize how excited I am to share everything with him.

I stare off into the darkness, keeping a look out for a stroller. The butterflies in my belly are flapping their wings, but I feel a lot lighter and more hopeful just seeing Vito's text.

Maybe it's time to stop fighting the story and let my future write itself for once.

Juniper falls sound asleep within minutes of us pulling out of the college parking lot, so Vito and I don't talk much on the drive back to the hotel.

He drives, and I stare out the window, lost in lots of fast-moving thoughts.

When we get back to the hotel, I lift Junie out of the back seat and carry her inside. I put her to bed, then join Vito in the living room. He's standing in the kitchen, tapping a text into his phone when I get back.

"Hey," he says, looking happy to see me. The sight of him fills my chest with a sudden burst of warmth.

I walk up to him, and he pulls me into his arms.

"How's it feel?" he asks. "Tomorrow night at this time, you'll be tucking Junie into bed in her very own room."

I hold him close and nod against his shoulder. "I almost can't believe it. I'm feeling so many things... especially tonight."

He takes my hand and leads me to the couch. "You want to talk about it?"

I look down at our hands and open my mouth, but where do I start? I don't know what I should say first.

It was great meeting your stripper ex-wife? Or, your stripper ex-wife is a great teacher?

"Eden, can I start?" Vito's staring me in the face, his lips parted. "I want to hear everything you want to say, but I need to get some shit off my chest."

I nod, relieved that he wants to talk. I still need some time with my feelings before I can even compose a coherent sentence.

"I'm sorry you had to meet my ex-wife that way. Super fucking awkward and I hope she didn't put you off that college completely."

I smile and shake my head. "No, she's pretty great, actually," I admit.

Vito nods, but then he takes both my hands in his. "Eden, you're more than pretty great. You have a lot of big shit ahead. I want to be a part of it. I want to be a part of your life."

We both chuckle and lace our fingers tighter.

"I don't know if you need a label, boyfriend, girl-friend, whatever. I'm falling for you, Eden. I think you're the most gorgeous, kindest, amazing woman. And I just wanted to be clear that Michelle is my past. I'd really like for you to be my future. You know what I mean?"

I silence him by leaning forward and kissing him

lightly on the lips. "I want that too," I tell him and scoot closer, tucking against his chest.

He rests his chin on the top of my head.

"I want to tell you something," I start. "I'm afraid it might change how you feel about me, and if it does, I'd rather know now before I get in any deeper. Because I'm falling for you too." I pull away then, feeling worried that Vito might reject me for what I'm about to admit. "It shook me a lot, meeting Michelle," I say, looking down into my lap. "But she's beautiful and smart and super fucking nice. I would have rather she be this nasty bitch, but no, she was like someone I could be friends with."

Vito laughs. "Fucking small towns," he says. "Really living up to their reputations."

I sigh. "Yeah. But that's the thing. You and Michelle just didn't work, right? There was no other big secret or anything?"

Vito cups my chin and holds my face so our eyes meet. "No," he says firmly, his voice low and sincere. He releases my chin and shakes his head. "I don't have secrets, Eden. Not one. What you see with me is what you get, for better or worse."

I swallow hard and realize how damning what I'm about to share is. "Well, I have more secrets," I say. "And if you can't forgive me for what I have done, I understand. Just…" Tears sting my eyes, and I clench my hands into fists so I don't cry. "Juniper's father," I say, looking down again. "He was married when I dated him. He was my boss. The owner of the company where I worked. He and his wife owned the business together, but she lives in New York City and handles East Coast development. I never actually met her during the two years I worked there."

I explain that the whole affair only lasted four months. That during that time, my boss insisted his wife was leaving him and that they had an understanding that he could date other people.

They ran a company that provided financing for films, so a divorce would have damaged their reputations and split their assets. He assured me they were married in name only. That was, until I told him I was pregnant.

"That's when I found out the marriage was very much real and not open or anything like that. I met his wife when she showed up at my desk with a team of lawyers and summoned me into a conference room." I choke back sobs, but the tears are flowing down my cheeks.

"Eden." Vito's voice is soft as he strokes the hair back from my face. "I'm sorry if meeting Michelle opened up those old wounds."

I shake my head. "It's inevitable," I explain. "Based on what went down when I got pregnant, I am pretty sure I was not the first executive assistant he played."

Vito's growl vibrates through my chest. "I'm so fucking sorry that happened to you. But I don't understand. Why would this change how I feel about you? If anything, I am fucking furious at what happened to you, and I want to make sure no one ever does anything to screw you over ever again."

"Seriously?" I wipe my face with both hands and face him. "Vito, you come from a huge, close-knit family. Your ex-wife is beautiful and talented, and there's no deep, dark secret there." I bark out a resentful laugh. "I had to sign a contract promising I would not submit my daughter's DNA to any of those genealogy sites until her eighteenth birthday."

"What?" he asks, sounding as shocked as I am pissed. "Why the fuck not?"

I give him a sad look. "I'm sure her father doesn't want her finding all the other siblings he's got running around out there in the world. If the kids start comparing the deals they got…" I shake my head.

I'm quiet then. I'm hoping the details I've shared haven't in any way compromised the confidentiality agreement I signed.

"I'm not supposed to talk about any of this," I explain. "But Vito, I want to talk about this shit to you. I want to trust you with everything. I want you. I just hope after everything I've said, you still want me."

Vito stands from the couch and pulls me to stand beside him. "Babe," he breathes before pressing his lips to mine, "if anything, I want you even more."

CHAPTER 13
VITO

I SLIDE my hands into the back pockets of Eden's jeans and press her hips firmly against mine. "Babe," I groan, "I want you more than anything."

She whimpers against my lips, opening her mouth so my tongue can tease hers. I feel her lace her hands around my waist as our kiss increases. We're like starving people feasting on our last meal. It's hot, it's furious, it's needy.

With Juniper always around, we haven't been able to do more than this in the weeks we've known each other, but tonight, I want more.

"Eden," I pant, palming her generous ass through the denim. "I want you so bad."

She pulls her face from mine, her cheeks blazing

pink. "I bought condoms," she whispers, giving me a grin. "They're in my bathroom."

I groan. That means she has to leave me to go into her bedroom, risking waking Juniper.

She laughs, and I point to the closed bedroom door behind which the sweetest little girl is sound asleep. "Think she'll wake up?"

She nods. "Oh, I'm a mama on a mission. I'll get this done." Before I know what she's doing, she's slipped out of my arms and is opening the bedroom door with the stealth of a ninja. I don't even hear the hinges creak as she disappears inside the bedroom and returns in what seems like ten seconds, gripping a box in her hands.

"We don't have to use them all," she says, one corner of her mouth curling up seductively. "But I wasn't going to tear this open in there."

I take the box from her and tear it open, freeing a sleeve of foil-wrapped condoms and dropping them on the coffee table. "We might need them all," I tease, watching as she wiggles her arms out of her sleeves and slips off her top.

She's wearing just her bra, but at the sight of her full tits, the blue veins streaking along the top of her creamy skin, my mouth drops open, and I just watch her.

"Fuck, you're gorgeous." I'm panting now, like someone who's never seen a tit before, but I don't care. Eden is sensual and soft, her curves thick and perfectly proportioned. I could probably come from just watching her undress, but I don't plan on losing control that soon. "Will she be okay?" I ask, jerking a thumb toward Eden's closed bedroom door.

Eden nods. "If she wakes up, we'll hear her. She can't get out of the pack and play, so she won't be able to open the door and surprise us."

I breathe a sigh of relief, then nod at Eden. "In that case, will you please take those fucking jeans off?"

She flashes me a smile and then unbuttons the top button. She works the zipper down and then shoves the fabric over her ample hips. She's wearing boy-cut underwear, a pair that's so sheer, I can see the shadow of her pubic hair through it.

"I want to see every inch of you." I pull her close to me and gently kiss her lips.

"Hmm, please." She closes her eyes, and I reach around her and unfasten the clasp. The flimsy fabric falls away, and I toss it on the end of the couch.

I squeeze my eyes shut as a spear of arousal spikes through my body, my legs going weak. "Fuck," I breathe.

Her breasts are large and soft, but when I trail the pads of my thumbs over her nipples, they go stiff and hard as pebbles. I pinch the tender flesh between my fingertips, and her shuddering gasp lets me know she likes how it feels.

She squirms under my touch, and I move her over to the couch. "On your back," I say, fumbling with the zipper of my jeans.

She obeys, lying on the couch as I settle my weight on top of her as best I can. "Am I crushing you?"

"I wouldn't mind if you did," she says, reaching up to stroke my hair away from my forehead.

"Tell me if you can't breathe," I say, then I lower my face to her cleavage. I start with one breast, sucking the entire nipple into my mouth and working the tip of my tongue over her peak until she gasps. She grips the back of my hair with her fingers and pushes my face into her chest.

"More," she whimpers.

I go feral when I hear that, and I clamp her nipple between my teeth and tug.

She goes weak, the pressure of her fingers in my hair slackening while she enjoys every second of my attention.

I suck and lick her nipple until she's writhing

beneath me, but then I stop and kiss her, trying to ignore the throb in my balls that's begging for release.

We kiss gently and wildly, tasting each other and savoring the first feel of our bare chests against each other. Eden must have incredibly sensitive nipples because while we're kissing, she's arching her back to press against the hairs on my chest.

"You feel so good," she murmurs against my mouth.

I wish I had words, pretty words to tell her how I feel right now. How seeing her like this beneath me makes me want to look into her eyes and just hold her, naked, for days. But those words will come later.

I move from lying on her to kneeling at her feet, and grab the waistband of her underwear before pulling them off. I spread her legs wide and lean back down so our chests touch.

She tightens her long legs around my waist, pulling our hips closer together, and my cock jumps in my briefs. "I want you, but my body's not..."

I instantly know her run-in with Michelle is toying with her brain.

I silence her with a soft kiss on the lips. "Everything about you is perfect," I tell her. "I'm falling for you, Eden. Flaws and all." I look down at her body and growl. "But everything I'm seeing is perfect. Flawless and perfect."

She nods and blinks self-consciously before pulling my head to her chest.

I rest my face between her breasts and groan. "You're killing me, babe. I mean, in the best way, but…"

She laughs, and we hold each other for a minute. "I'm good," she whispers. "Thank you."

"No, E, thank you." I move back to the end of the couch and tug the panties over her hips, down her thighs, and set them on the coffee table. "For this."

I grip the insides of both her thighs and run my hands from her knees to her pussy. While she gets used to my touch, I lower myself as best I can to fit on the couch, but it's not going to work. "New plan," I say, getting up from the couch and reaching out my hand.

I help her to standing, yank a blanket off a nearby chair, and drop it on the carpeted floor like a picnic blanket. "Now, I'll be able to eat your pussy without wrenching my damn back."

She laughs and lies back on the blanket, opening her legs to me. "You're so safety-conscious," she teases. "At least you're trained if one of us gets hurt."

"The only pain you're going to feel is the kind

you want," I promise as I settle between her legs. I hook my hands under her knees and bend her legs so her feet are on the floor, her knees falling open.

Then I lie on my belly and place one hand on her abdomen. With the other hand, I feel my way through her trimmed hair until I feel her drenched lips.

She sucks air as I touch her, and I feel the sound as though she hummed it against my balls. I'm so hard I might just come against the fucking floor. But I quickly distract myself from the demands of my cock by stroking every inch of Eden's middle.

She is gripping the blanket with her hands and tightening her knees, closing her legs around my head, but I push them open again, continuing to work my thumb until she begs me to fill her.

"Vito, I need you inside me. Please." When she finally says the words, I reach for a condom, tear that thing open like there's a winning lottery ticket inside, and shed my briefs so I can sheathe up.

I kneel down on the blanket and settle my weight over her. "You want it like this?"

She nods but then says, "And behind."

"In your ass?" I ask, trying to clarify.

Her eyes widen, and she shakes her head, her gorgeous, soft hair shifting over the blanket. "No, I mean I want you behind me."

I chuckle and she giggles. "That too," I say as I lower my weight and press the tip of my dick to her pussy.

She is wet and sweet, and when I'm fully inside her, she widens her legs, and I swear to fuck I see stars.

I thrust inside her, my hips and thighs burning with the effort, a sheen of sweat gathering on my forehead and chest.

She rolls her hips, lifting to meet my thrusts with her own. My arms burn as I support my weight, thrusting deep inside her while I watch her breasts bounce and her beautiful lips move as she moans.

"I want you to come," I tell her, and her eyes fly open.

"I will," she promises. "But I want this to last."

I shake my head with a grin. "Babe, I promise this won't be the last time, but I can't hold out for long."

She giggles and turns a bit to her side. "Can we flip over?" she asks.

"Fuck yeah." I pull out of her, and her groan matches the disappointed grunt I make at the loss of contact. I check the condom's all good, watching as she gets on all fours.

Once she's kneeling, I settle behind her and grip her thighs. She reaches between her legs to guide my cock inside, but as soon as I'm deep, she lifts her ass in the air, pressing into me. I hold her hips, watching her ass bounce against me as I thrust.

"Vito, oh yes," she moans.

It's the best kind of yes because as soon as she starts, I feel it. I feel her pussy tighten around my cock, and she muffles a shriek into the blanket. "Oh my God!" she yells, shoving her ass against me, writhing and grinding and panting through her orgasm.

The second she's done, I'm done for, and I give in to the climax that shakes my legs and drains me of every ounce of pent-up need.

I collapse against her bare back and plant kisses along her spine until we both crash onto the blanket. I cuddle her close, both of us breathless and sweating and naked and flushed.

"Are you good?" I mutter, tightening my arms around her.

Her face is pressed against my damp pectoral, and she barely moves her face as she mumbles against my skin. "Great."

We hold each other for a few minutes until we both doze off.

I wake up early the next morning in my bed back at home, my morning wood wishing like hell I had Eden by my side. I shoot her a text before I roll out.

Me: I know it's early. Thinking about you. Can't wait to christen your new house.

Ordinarily with a woman, I'd overthink what to do the day after we first hooked up.

But with Eden, I am oddly at ease. Maybe it helps because I'm going to see her today at the closing. I told her I'd be there for the final walk-through of the house and to help with Juniper while she signed all the paperwork.

I'm not nervous at all, but I am oddly excited. The house isn't mine, but I can't help thinking that it's a place where Eden will make a home for herself and her daughter.

And if there's room in that house, in her new life, for me, well... I'm not going to get too far ahead of myself.

But I know what I feel. It's not just the fucking fantastic sex, her killer body, or the fact that she's a sweetheart. Something about Eden feels right. Hanging out with Juniper alone last night never once felt like work. I never once checked the time, counting down the minutes until Eden came back to take her off my hands.

Sometimes, as much as I love my nieces and nephews, they are exhausting. I try to be the patient uncle, but it's hard to play the games they want, to remind them to wash their hands, to break up arguments, and to manage them every single second.

I'd been kind of reconsidering whether I even wanted kids of my own because, while they are amazing at times, the grind of keeping four little humans alive is more than I could fathom. I was settling into a comfortable shell until I met Eden.

Happy alone.

As happy as I could be with my work. Lost in my own little cocoon of safety in my parents' house. Now I'm wondering if, with the right person and the right kid, the worries, fears, and the risk aren't more than worth it.

My phone buzzes with a text and I grab it, expecting to hear from Eden. But the text is from a number I haven't seen in years.

Michelle: Hey V, it's Michelle. I don't know if this is still your number, but if it is, I thought I'd see if you were free for a quick coffee today? If you're working, let me know when you're off.

I look down at the message, dumbfounded.

I haven't heard a word from Michelle in five freaking years. Now she wants to grab coffee? I rub my face and jump out of bed, ignoring the text for now.

I storm into the shower and let the hot water clear my head. It's early, but Michelle no doubt remembers my schedule and my habits. I'm not sure if it's a good or bad thing that I haven't changed.

As I wash my hair, I think about the last five years. How lost I've been. How close I've come time and time again to reaching for what I thought I wanted, only to be passed over for the promotion, if I was even considered at all.

After I'm dressed, I look at my phone with disgust. I don't know what Michelle wants. Maybe nothing. Maybe something. But I don't think I can move forward with Eden until I kick all the ghosts of my past to the curb.

I text Michelle back and head downstairs, hoping I am not making a jackass-stupid move.

Michelle's office is in a nice area of Star Falls. No one is sitting at the reception desk, so I stand there and look around, unsure where to go. After a couple minutes, a man in a suit that probably cost more than my truck payment rushes out to the front.

"Good morning," he says. "Sorry to keep you waiting. Our receptionist is tied up. Do you have an appointment?"

I look the guy over and shrug. "Yeah, I guess. I'm here to see Michelle." I look down at the jeans and flannel shirt I'm wearing and suddenly feel all the old shit come back.

How I was never enough for Michelle. The way she always wanted me to dress better. But I don't have a lot of time to worry about it because Michelle comes through the reception door herself then.

"Vito." She walks right up to me and gives me a very real hug.

I clumsily hug her back, regretting every idiotic thought that brought me here. "Hey," I say, stepping out of the hug as soon as I can.

"John," she says to the guy in the suit, "I'm going to take Vito back to my office. Would you hang out up front until Gennie is back?"

The guy nods, looking me over with a hint of suspicion. I follow Michelle back into her office, looking at the pristine carpet tiles as I follow her. Being here alone with Michelle feels like I'm betraying Eden, even if my intention is to listen to what she has to say and get the fuck out of here as fast as I can.

Eden's final walk-through is at noon, so I have less than an hour before I have to pick her up, and that's about ten times longer than I plan on staying.

Michelle's name is posted on a plaque outside the door, and she scans herself in using a keycard.

"Fancy," I say, following her into the spacious, light-filled room.

She nods. "For client security. I only have a few advisers here, and we keep our private offices locked."

She motions for me to sit down, then pulls up an app on her phone to order us coffee. "Still the same?" she asks, smiling. "Or do you want something different? I don't want to assume nothing has changed since we last saw each other."

I'm feeling more and more irritated by the second. If she orders coffee, that means I'm stuck here for at least fifteen minutes until it gets here. I'm itching to leave so bad I can't keep my hands still.

"I'm good," I say, waving her off. "I've got someplace to be, so…"

She cocks her chin at me and frowns. "I'm sorry. I thought you…" She firms her lips, punches in an order, then sets her phone down. She sits behind her desk and motions for me to have a seat. I do, figuring the sooner we get through this, the better.

She leans back in her chair and looks at me warmly. "Vito, maybe I was stupid for inviting you here. I thought it could be good to talk a bit."

I nod. "Go ahead and talk."

Even as I say it, I hate that I sound like a moody teenager. I'm a grown fucking man, and this woman loved me once.

"Okay, let me just say this," I tell her. "I heard you were back in town, but I'm seeing someone I really care about now, and I just..." I shrug. "I don't know what there really is to say."

Michelle stuns me by laughing and leaning forward on her desk. "Thank you," she says. "Thanks for being honest. That's literally all I wanted."

She sighs and then leans back. "Maybe it's me who needs to talk. So, can you give me five minutes? If you don't like what I have to say, you can leave and tell me to fuck off, and I won't bother you again."

I nod, feeling a tiny bit less grumpy. "Shoot," I tell her. "Floor's yours."

She gives me a big smile. "Well, you probably heard I came back to Star Falls to help my grandfather. He's in that memory care place up on Devon and Wilson Drive."

I nod. "I heard. I'm sorry things have gotten rough. Your gramps was always good to me."

"You deserved it," she says warmly. "You're a wonderful man, Vito."

Alarm bells like a five-alarm fire sound in my ears. Where the fuck is this going?

"I'll cut to the chase," she says. "You know we didn't work out for reasons. But I have no hard feelings, and I hope you don't either. I'm dating someone now who I've been with for almost four years." She turns a picture frame on her desk to show me a picture of her in a bikini on a beach with some guy wearing orange floral trunks. He looks like a douchebag to me, but Michelle looks happy, so I just nod.

Her voice is soft as she explains. "He's a lawyer. We're doing the long-distance thing for a few months while he's working up a case that should go to trial by the end of the year. Once that's over, he's going to spend half his time here in Star Falls with me."

"That's great, Michelle. I'm happy for you." I rub my hands on my thighs, ready to bolt. "I hope it all works out."

I'm about to jump out of my seat when there is a soft knock at the door. Michelle waves at a woman who I assume is the receptionist. She comes in carrying a cardboard drink caddy with two coffees on it.

"Gennie, thank you." Michelle introduces me to the receptionist, who is enormously pregnant. "I'd like you to meet Vito Bianchi."

I shake her hand and look at her face. "Are you by any chance related to the fire chief?"

Gennie grins. "I'm married to his oldest, Rory." She points to her belly. "His."

Something about the fact that Gennie is related to my chief sets me at ease. I feel a lot less out of place and under the microscope, but the chief's daughter-in-law leaves and I'm again alone with Michelle.

"I got you the usual," Michelle says, shoving a paper cup across her desk at me. "But you don't have to drink it."

I grab the cup and take a sip. I look down at the plastic lid as I mutter, "You remember how I like my coffee after all this time."

Michelle nods. "I loved you, Vito. And I still want the best for you, even if we've both moved on." She sips her drink, then continues. "I like Eden a lot," she says. "The admissions counselor called me this morning to see how the classroom visit went. I think Eden has a bright future."

I shrug, not sure I like the idea of my new girl-friend following in the footsteps of my ex-wife. "Yeah. Eden's great," I say guardedly.

Michelle looks thoughtful as she finally lays it all out on the table. "Eden is actually the reason I wanted to talk to you."

I meet her eyes over my hot coffee and brace myself. I wish I had some antacid. If it's a Michelle idea, I know it's going to burn.

I check the time and sigh. "All right," I say, resigned to listening.

That's all I have to do.

Then, like she said, I can block her and leave the past where it belongs.

CHAPTER 14
EDEN

TODAY MIGHT JUST BE the worst day of my life.

I stagger into the kitchenette of the hotel, feeling like I got hit by a truck. Sharp knocking at the door nearly takes the breath from my lungs as I run to the door to open it before whoever it is brings the two seconds of peace I've had to a miserable end.

I don't even check the peephole, just yank open the door and squint into the sunlight.

"Today's the day." My aunt Shirley is beaming, her arms wide open.

I step outside into the sunlight and let the door close behind me. I wince at the noise and squint, a thousand little needles pricking behind my eyes.

"I know, but it couldn't be off to a worse start." I

lean into Aunt Shirley's arms and rest my head against her shoulder.

"Uh-oh." Sassy steps out of our hug and peers into my face like she can read the bad news in my eyes. "Spill it, kiddo. What happened? Isn't today the closing? Did the seller back out?"

I shake my head. "No, thank goodness. No. Everything is happening." I rub my forehead and sigh. "It's Juniper. She's got to be cutting another tooth or something." I tell my aunt about one of the worst nights we've had. "She had a low fever yesterday around lunch, but she didn't seem bothered until about midnight. She woke me up screaming bloody murder. I mean, bloody murder."

I tell her how I couldn't calm Junie down. I was so worried about noise traveling through the thin walls of the hotel and waking every single guest that I put her in the car and tried to calm her while keeping the screaming inside the confines of my vehicle. That didn't work, so I started driving.

"I actually got stopped by a Star Falls officer for sitting on the side of the road with my car idling," I say, shaking my head. "He was pretty sympathetic when I explained what was going on and showed him my hotel key and stuff." I rub my eyes.

Junie finally crashed at four in the morning, but

then she woke up at seven super cranky and whiny. I fed her breakfast and just got her back down for what I hope is a decent nap.

Aunt Sassy's right on time, so it's got to be around eleven. "I don't think I slept more than two hours last night." I frown and rub my burning eyes. "I just hope this isn't a sign of things to come."

Sassy crosses her arms over her chest and shakes her head. A soft cloud of her perfume greets me, and it's hard not to smile. She smells like home, like a grandma. "If anything," she says, "this is a clear sign it's long past time you get that baby into your own house." She looks truly undone and starts talking really fast. "Honey, damn it. You should have called me. Even in the middle of the night, I could have come by and helped."

To be honest, I'd thought about that. Aunt Sassy lives in an apartment, so I couldn't just show up with a screaming toddler at midnight and make enemies with all her neighbors.

And then, of course, I thought about Vito. But I know he's back on shift tomorrow, and there was no way I was going to wake up his parents and mess up his sleep schedule.

"I managed," I say quietly.

"Eden. Baby." Sassy grabs my hands and holds

them tightly in hers. "I want you to hear me when I say this." She presses her hot-pink lips together, the fine lines around her mouth deepening as she frowns. "You are family, Eden. Flesh and blood. You are not alone. I don't care if it's the middle of the night and I have a hot guy in my bed. You knock on that door, and you ask for help."

She shakes her head and blinks fast, sniffling like she might cry. "I was never able to be there when you were a girl. When you could have used someone close by." She releases my hands and clutches her hands in front of her chest. "I wanted to, Eden. I wanted to be there for you. Please let me do that now. Let me be there for you, sweetheart."

The tears are flowing before she even finishes speaking. I need time to accept that I am not alone anymore. That there are people who don't just want to be part of my life; there are people who would willingly shoulder my burdens.

"Auntie," I say, trying to force a half smile as I wipe my nose with the back of my hand. "A hot guy? Is there something we should talk about?"

My aunt snorts. "That ship's sailed, sweetheart, but you get my point."

I wrap an arm around her shoulder and point

toward the door. "Let's get inside. I've got to get presentable before the closing."

I reach for the doorknob and realize the hotel door locked behind us. I pat my back pocket for my keycard, but I don't feel it.

"Oh, sweet baby Jesus," I sigh. I listen for screaming from inside the room, but it's quiet. "I think I left my keycard inside with Juniper."

"Oh, holy mother." Sassy looks terrified and starts tearing through her purse for her phone. "Should I call 9-1-1? Should we break the window?" She starts looking around, and I hope like hell she's not about to pick up a rock.

"Auntie," I say calmly. "After last night, I am sure that if Juniper were awake, we'd hear her. You stay here and keep watch. I'll go to the front desk. I've been staying here long enough that I'm sure they know who I am and will give me another key."

I head over toward the lobby, unable to stop myself from casting a look backward to make sure my aunt isn't about to send a potted plant through a window.

I have to say, though, it brings me a lot of comfort to know I have someone in my life who would destroy public property if my daughter's safety were at risk.

I hustle over to the lobby, smoothing my hair and wiping my cheeks. I have no makeup on and probably look like a swamp troll, but as long as I look like the woman they know is staying in that room, they should let me in.

When I get to the lobby, the girl at the front desk is on the phone. She holds up a hand with a smile and lets me know she'll be right with me.

Maybe the next time Junie has a meltdown, or I have a fire or need anything…maybe I won't force myself to go through it alone.

And then, I hear his voice. "Hey, gorgeous."

I throw myself into Vito's arms and practically smash my lips against his. "I'm a mess," I warn him. "I didn't sleep, I'm not wearing makeup, and I haven't showered since yesterday morning."

He stops my words with a kiss. "You're perfect," he says. "Sassy sent me in here." He holds the extra keycard I gave him a few days ago between his fingers. "Let's get back to your room. I had to wrestle a concrete block out of your aunt's hand, but she made no promises."

The final walk-through and the closing both went off without a hitch. Robert actually hugged Vito and me after handing over the keys. It was a bittersweet moment for him, and I promised him that we'd make some beautiful new memories in the place he's called home.

I'm standing inside the house when I check my phone again, even though my aunt assured me that Juniper is fine. Fussy, but no more freak-outs. That's when the real work starts.

Vito has recruited his brother Franco, his father Mario, and, of course, Lucia to help move over all the essential stuff from the hotel. The afternoon is a blur of trips back and forth, messages, phone calls, and a hell of a lot of sweating.

By dinnertime, I have furniture in Juniper's room, all my stuff moved out of the hotel, and a couch in the living room to sleep on tonight.

"Hun, what time is the official move tomorrow?" Lucia is wearing the cutest little pair of reading glasses, which she has moved from a beaded chain around her neck onto the end of her nose.

"Around nine," I tell her.

"I'll be there," Franco says. "Text me the address."

"You sure you don't want to stay? I can order pizza," I offer.

Franco shakes his head. "Nah, I'm going to meet Chloe at the bookstore to grab my baby girl. I'm good, sweetheart. We'll see you tomorrow." Franco hugs his brother and calls out a goodbye to his parents, his voice echoing through the mostly empty house.

Lucia and Mario are next to leave.

"We'll bring food tomorrow once you're more settled," Lucia promises. Her eyes grow misty, and she stands up on her tippy toes but I still have to bend down a bit so she can hold my cheeks. "I'm so happy for you, Eden. This is going to make the most beautiful home."

Mario kisses me goodbye and claps Vito on the shoulder. "See you in a couple days, son." Then he turns to kiss my cheek. "And I'll be back tomorrow." He leans down to whisper in my ear. "Lucia already decided you need a dog for that yard. I don't know how long I can hold her off."

Sassy comes into the kitchen with Junie. "Getting dark out there," she calls out. "And I think this little one needs some dinner."

"Do you want to stay, Auntie? Let me buy you dinner."

Shirley shakes her head and holds up a hand. "I got to get these knees in a hot bath. I'm on lunch service tomorrow." She kisses my daughter on both cheeks and blows raspberries against her neck. "You let your mama sleep tonight, you hear?"

Junie giggles and leans her face against Sassy's velvet leggings.

"Thanks, Sassy," Vito says, hugging my aunt goodbye.

"You." She wags a finger at Vito. "I love you, you know that? And you're damn lucky this niece of mine didn't meet Benito first."

Vito waves her off and laughs as he throws an arm around my shoulders, and I melt into his side. We stand at the front door together, watching as the last of our family pulls away.

True happiness always seemed like something other people grabbed so easily. But now, the life I always wanted isn't just close. I'm in it. And I never dreamed it could feel this good.

CHAPTER 15
VITO

THE FIRST MONTH after Eden moves into her house goes by in a blur. I spend almost every night at Eden's place, except the nights when I'm working. It's not that I've moved in; it's just that so much shit comes up with a new house. Furniture to be moved, boxes needing to be unpacked. Eden has rearranged the kitchen pantry so many times, I don't know where anything is from one day to the next. But I don't care. She's over the goddamn moon every day. This home has brought her so much pleasure, and I am just happy to be a part of it.

And it's hard to deny that I'm becoming a bigger part of all of it—not just the house—I'm talking Eden's and Juniper's lives.

Tonight, we agreed that Eden would take the night

off from organizing cabinets and we would just sit back and enjoy the place.

I stretch out and rest my head back against the cushions. The TV is on, but the volume is low. I'm not too interested in watching anything. I just want to spend time with Eden when we're not deciding whether heavy canned goods should go on a low shelf or a high shelf. Don't get me wrong. I love the process, but tonight, I don't want to watch her alphabetize soup.

She comes out of the kitchen with two glasses of water. She leaves our drinks on the coffee table and then collapses next to me on the couch. She's quiet for a minute, and I tap her on the thigh with my fingers.

"Go on," I urge.

"What?" Her lips curl into a knowing smile.

"I know what you're thinking. Just say it so we can move on."

She opens her mouth to say it, and I time my words so we both say it at the same time. "Can you believe this is really my house?"

"You're the worst," she says, looping her arms around my neck. She kisses my ear. "I'm not that predictable."

"Eden," I say, tilting my head so our faces are

close. "You totally are, and I love seeing you this happy."

She kisses me lightly on the lips, then snuggles against my side. I put an arm around her shoulders and pull her close. "Your mother wants me to get a dog," she says. "She has almost got me convinced."

I shake my head. "I do not get between Lucia and her rescues. That includes you."

"Hey." Eden elbows me. "But I guess I deserve that. You know your mom offered to give me cooking lessons."

"Better you than me," I say. "Ma and Pops are great cooks. I am a great microwaver."

We hold each other tightly and watch the images cross the TV.

"A dog could be good protection," she says quietly. "For when you're not here."

My housewarming gift to Eden was a video security system. She has cameras all around the property, and I set up the text alerts to message both my phone and hers if anything triggers the sensors.

Star Falls is safe, but you can never be too safe. Even if I've mostly been notified that she has an active family of raccoons living out back. Definitely one point in the pro column if she's thinking about getting a dog.

"Do you not feel safe here?" I ask, growing concerned. "When you're by yourself?"

She nods, her soft hair rustling against the fabric of my shirt. "It's not that so much. It's just... I don't know. This place feels different when you're not here, like something's missing."

I lift her chin so I can look her in the eye. "Babe, we talked about this. This is your house. Your first home. You've got to spend time in it. You don't need anyone else claiming a closet or half your bed. Isn't that what you want? Reorganizing everything? Making this the perfect place for you and Junie?"

She shrugs. "Yeah. That makes sense. I know I need to do things for myself."

"No." I shake my head. "That's not what I'm saying. I'm saying this is your house. Your dream. I want you to have a little time to enjoy it. I don't need to have my name on the mailbox to feel at home here."

She's quiet, but then she sniffs hard, and her cheeks grow red. "Is it because you don't want me? Are we too much?"

I move so I'm sitting at the edge of the couch and can see right into Eden's eyes. "Are you serious?" I ask quietly. "What are you saying?"

Eden's voice is shaking. "I know we've only

known each other a few months, but would you want to move in here with us?"

The breath catches in my throat at her question. "That's a massive step, babe. Is that what you want?"

Her face is expressionless. "I want to know what you want, Vito. I need you to just tell me the truth." She looks down at her hands. "I feel like ever since I moved into this place, you've pulled away a bit."

I reach for her hands, and we lace our fingers together tightly. "Eden, I'm not just here for the good times. I'm not that guy, the one who bolts the second things get boring or serious or hard." I bite down on my lower lip, trying to find the right words. "I want to be here for you, no matter what you're doing."

It's then I realize that I have completely and totally forgotten about Michelle's offer.

"Shit," I say and slap my forehead. "Babe, I'm a fucking moron. You see what I mean? I forgot to give you a message." I lean back against the couch and sigh. "I've got to take ten steps back. So, on the day of your closing, Michelle asked if we could talk."

Eden's body immediately stiffens, and I know I have only a couple seconds before I shatter her trust in me.

"Now, look, I'll show you my phone, babe. That

was the only time I've talked to Michelle in five years since our divorce except, of course, for the day we ran into her at the college." I reach for my phone, which is sitting on the coffee table, but Eden stops me with a hand on my arm.

"I don't need to see. I trust you more than I've ever trusted anyone." The words are coming out of her mouth, but they don't quite match the look in her eyes.

That's not good enough for me.

"Uh-huh," I say, shaking my head. I pick up the phone and swipe the screen. "I want you to trust me completely."

She smiles, a sad, thin thing. "I do trust you completely, but it means everything that you would offer to show me proof."

"How the fuck did we get on this topic?" I ask, crinkling my brow.

"You said you forgot to give me a message," Eden reminds me.

"Right." I scroll to the last text and show it to Eden. "Michelle asked me to give you a message the day the house closed, and I seriously forgot. It left my mind the second I walked out of there, and now I don't even know if the offer still stands."

"Offer?" She sits up straight and now does peer over my shoulder as I text.

Me: I'm a fucking idiot, but that's not news to you. I completely forgot to mention your offer to Eden. She bought a house, and with all the moving and shit, it slipped my mind. I'm with her now. It's been a month, though, so before I tell her, I just want to ask if the offer is still open?

I click send and turn to Eden. "I'm going to tell you anyway," I say, "but I don't know what I'm going to do if shit's changed and I screwed you out of a great thing."

She looks at me, her beautiful eyes squinting, as if she's trying to read the honesty there in my face.

"First of all, I'm so sorry it slipped my mind, and I didn't tell you sooner. I get so focused on work, and then when I'm not on the job, I am all in whatever else I'm doing. And for the last month, that's been you."

She giggles and I nod.

"After you took Michelle's class, she had me out to her office. Said she thought you were really smart and that with some guidance, you could do great things." I shake my head. "Now that I'm saying it out loud, I wonder if part of me wanted to forget the offer. Wanted to put as much distance between Michelle and you as I possibly could." I meet her eyes, and there's no hiding how I'm feeling when I say this. I feel the emotion like a physical pain in my chest. "Her receptionist is pregnant. She's actually married to my chief's son." I grin, but then the seriousness of what I have to say comes back to haunt my words. "Michelle wanted to know if you wanted the job. You can work either part time or full time covering for the receptionist while she's out on maternity leave. It's a paid job, of course, and you can try doing what she does for a few months before you spend the money committing to college and a degree in some financial shit."

The look on Eden's face transforms from playful to stone serious.

Before I can say anything, my phone rings. The caller ID shows it's Michelle. "You mind if I talk to her?" I ask.

She nods, and I click to connect the call.

"Hey," I say.

"Hey." Her voice is loud and bright. I notch down the volume a bit so she doesn't wake Juniper. "I'm good. Is Eden with you?"

I nod at her, and Eden greets her. "Um, yes. Hi, Michelle."

"Hey." She laughs. "You know I gave you my

number in class that day, and then I spoke to Vito about the job. When I didn't hear from either of you for a month, I figured that was your way of telling the ex to go fuck herself and mind her own business."

I immediately set the record straight. "Michelle, this was all me. You know my memory and how I get when I'm working."

"Don't worry about it," she says. "I do know, and I wouldn't blame either one of you if you weren't interested in anything that had to do with me."

Eden is leaning forward, looking really conflicted.

"So, no pressure, but I just saw your text. My receptionist is officially going on leave in two weeks. Unless she goes into labor sooner. She's a little flexible on her date, but she wants some time to fix up the nursery a bit more before the baby comes. If Eden is interested, we can try to get her in as soon as possible to do some training with Gennie. I'll handle the rest once Gennie's off."

"Here," I say, picking up my phone and taking it off speaker. "Michelle, I'm going to give my phone to Eden. Let you two talk. I literally just mentioned this two minutes ago, so she may have questions."

I offer the phone to Eden, and she takes it. Then she stands and paces through the living room while she talks.

I get up and wander back to the bathroom, wasting time while they talk.

After a couple of minutes, I head back to the living room. Eden is sitting on the couch, looking down at my phone in her hands.

"You good? All done?" I ask.

She nods, so I come join her on the couch. "You didn't have to leave," she says.

I hold up my hand. "This is between you two now. I was just the messenger."

Eden sets the phone on the coffee table and gives me a confused look. "I don't know what to think," she admits. "It's weird, right? Your ex-wife offering me a job?"

"I'm sure Michelle is excited to meet someone who has an interest in what she does. It would only be weird if you…" I have to stop myself from saying the words.

"If I what?" she presses.

Ah, fuck. I can't get away with not saying it now. I've gone this far. I drag a hand through my hair and tug it at the roots. "I don't want to lose you, Eden. I don't want you to go to work for Michelle and then realize that I'm not good enough for you." I look her in the eye. "I've been through that once, and babe, I don't want to be your rebound guy. I don't want to be the guy you lean on until you find something better."

Eden's face sets into a mask of pure anger. I don't think I've ever seen her like this.

"Something better? You think I would ever find someone better than you?" She stands up and paces the living room, pointing an angry finger at me. "All this time, I've been feeling like a second-class citizen, worried that you're going to get sick of me. I don't have a family and a thousand siblings. I don't cook like your father does or want to stay home and raise kids like your mom did. When are you going to realize how damaged I am and just leave me?"

She's breathing hard, her face is flushed bright red, but I can tell there's sadness right under the surface of the pain.

I stand and cross the living room, taking her in my arms. "I feel like we need to talk. Really talk," I say. I lead her back to the couch, and we sit together, our hands locked. "I don't care if you can't cook. My brother owns a restaurant, and my parents always have way too much food around." I lift her hands to my lips and kiss her knuckles. "What I love about you is that you're real. You're flawed. I am too. You know that. I'd rather wear pajamas than pants. You don't expect me to be anything but what I am. You accept my work schedule, my sleep schedule. What I'm afraid of is that changing."

She squeezes my hands tight. "We're both going to change over time, at least somewhat," she says. "I'm a single mom. I come from a really messed-up family. I don't want to make the same mistakes my parents did. I want to be a different person in five years and maybe even an even more different person five years from that. I want more in life."

Something in my chest breaks open when her voice trembles.

"Listen to me." I cup her entire face in my hands. "You're everything. The way you love your daughter. The way you love me." I lean forward and rest my forehead against hers. "I want you to be happy, Eden, and if you want this job, you've got to take it. I want to support you in everything you want to try. I just don't want you to outgrow me."

We're quiet as the honesty of what we've said fills the space between us. I know too well there are no guarantees in life or love.

I don't know what I need from her. Maybe just for her to understand. Maybe that's all we can promise each other. At least right now.

"I don't know what to say," she admits. Her beautiful eyes well with tears. "I want to grow with you. Not away from you."

"All right. So, let's tackle one thing at a time. Do you want the job?" I finally ask. "You think it's the right thing for you?"

She nods slowly. "It sounds perfect. I can cover for Gennie for a few months. If I don't like the field, I'll find out before I waste money on tuition or student loans. I'm going to need support, though. Babysitting and someone to come home to so I can share stories about my day. I want the job, Vito, but I want you too. I want you to share it all with me. That's the only way we won't grow apart, if we're doing it all together. But I know it's a lot. I'm a work in progress, but I'm a package deal. Me and Juniper. Do you think you can handle us all the time?"

I almost can't say the words. I wish like hell Junie were awake so I could hold both of my girls in my arms. "It feels like something is missing not having this conversation with Junie right here."

I blink fast, and Eden reaches out a hand to stroke my cheek. "That's how I know..." she says, tears streaming down her cheeks. She smiles and says, "See? You're already the man I want and the father figure Junie deserves."

We grab each other then and cling together in a

tight hug. I bury my face in the length of her hair and just breathe her in.

She's younger than me, but this woman is smart. She knows herself. She understands that life hands you pain and opportunity, and somehow when it's all bundled together, you've got to make the decision to be happy.

Everything with Eden is an easy decision.

I don't have to decide to be happy with Eden. It's as if just being close to her makes every minute, every day, good.

In a weird way, I already feel like we're family. It's like our circumstances are just catching up to that reality.

"Can I say something?" I ask, pulling away just enough that I can whisper in her ear.

"Only if I can ask you something after."

"I love you, Eden. You are so damn easy to love. And I love your daughter too. I love what we have, and I'm in this, no matter how scared I am." I kiss her lips, a soft kiss wet with our shared tears.

"Move in here?" she asks. "Live with us, Vito."

I'm quiet as I think about it. I know what my answer is. I feel like I have always known this was coming. Is it possible I've known someplace deep down ever since the days she invited me to look at houses?

I moved back in with my parents after Michelle left, and over the years, it's been easier to stay there than it would have been to think about trying something new.

"I have a few conditions," I tell her. "I'm going to pay rent and half of all the costs—groceries, baby shit, and everything else. I'm going to carry my weight. In fact, more than my share of it. I make more than you right now, and I want to help make the money you have last longer so you have more options."

She doesn't say anything, but her face lights up. "Okay. What else?"

"This one I'm serious about," I tell her. "I need my own bedroom. Not for every day, but when I'm off shift and need to crash or when I just need to sleep. I don't want my schedule to fuck up yours. I'll sleep with you every chance I can get, but I need my own room so that we can both get space when we need it."

She's beaming now. "I have extra rooms."

I nuzzle my face against her neck. "So, you taking the job?" I ask.

"So, you moving in?" she asks.

"You going to rearrange everything in the whole house again now that I need a bedroom?" I ask.

"You know me so well," she whispers.

I groan, but then I pull her close. "There are parts of you I still need to know better."

"Which parts?" she asks.

And then I take her upstairs so I can show her.

CHAPTER 16
EDEN

I WAKE up before sunrise and my mind is spinning, but my first thoughts are of Junie. I squint at the image on the baby monitor on the bedside table.

Juniper is sound asleep, her little foot poking out from under a light blanket.

I roll over, and that's when it hits me. I'm alone in bed. I roll over and touch the cool sheets. Vito slept over last night, but he's not next to me.

My heart speeds up a bit at the thought that maybe he's not sleeping because he's not comfortable here.

Maybe he's having second thoughts about moving in. I take a deep breath and kick back the covers. I'm awake now, so I may as well face whatever this is. I am wearing my favorite paper-thin sleep tee with the wide, loose neck and soft pajama pants. I tiptoe down the stairs and find Vito in the kitchen, sitting in the eat-in nook with a sheet of paper and his phone in front of him.

"Babe." He brightens as soon as he sees me. "You're up early."

I pad over to the table and tuck into the cozy bench seat on the opposite side of where he's sitting. "I could say the same to you." A little bit of tension leaves my belly at the happy look on his face. "Are you okay?"

"Better than okay," he says. He gets up excitedly and scoots next to me on the bench. "Do you want coffee? I made some."

He grabs his empty mug and heads to the coffeepot, but then he shakes his head. "Shit. I drank the whole pot. I'll make more."

I get up from my seat and take the empty pot from him. "I'll do it. You tell me what's got you so excited that you're awake."

As I scoop up the grounds and fill the pot, Vito grabs the sheet of paper off the kitchen table. He sets the paper down on the counter and explains the notes he's made. "I've lived with my parents for the last five years and I'm a little ashamed to admit it now, but I've never paid my parents a penny in rent. I buy groceries every now and then, but..." He rubs the sexy scruff on his chin. "I've been a deadbeat son, but that means I've banked a ton of money." He points to a figure on the piece of paper. "I've been putting my money away and honestly never thought much about what I'd do with it. My truck's paid off. I've got no debt."

He meets my eyes, his bright and full of excitement. "We can use my savings to pay for your college. You don't have to worry about running out of the money in your trust. You can save all that for Juniper."

I shake my head and click the coffeemaker on. "Vito, I would never, ever let you pay my way through college."

He holds up a finger and smirks, his lips a full, sexy smile. "I thought you'd say that. So, I crunched some other numbers." He flips the paper over. "If we use my cash to make some upgrades to the house— new bathrooms upstairs, for example, we can throw some work at my buddies who do contract work on the side, so you know there'll be guys in the house you can trust. Then, when the work is done, you can get your house reappraised and maybe take out a loan against the equity."

I watch him in amazement. I've heard of things like this, but I have no idea how any of this stuff works. This is exactly why I want to learn. "Vito, but then your money is tied up in this house. What if something happens? I'll want to pay you back for the money you put into the house."

Vito drops his sheet of paper on the floor, then bends to pick it up. When he stands, his face looks strained. "Something happens? Eden, what's going to happen?"

I step closer to him and wrap my arms around his waist. "I don't want anything to happen, but I don't know about things like this. I don't ever want you to feel like I screwed you out of your money." I bite my lip, thinking about the vile, horrible things Nathan's wife said at the mediation.

Vito sets his phone and paper on the counter and grips my hips in both hands. "I'm not like Juniper's father. And I'm going to take all the time I need to show you I'm a very, very different man."

"You already have," I say, lowering my head to rest against his shoulder. "You've been up thinking about how to spend your money on me."

"On us," he corrects. He tugs my hips closer, and I can feel the firm lines of his body against mine. "When I wake up in the morning at my parents', I'm in their house. But when I woke up this morning, I was so excited I couldn't sleep. All I could picture was the playset we can put in the back for Juniper. The new bathrooms we can install."

"The dog run for my new puppy…" I say, a pleading note in my voice. "Because one screaming little animal in this house is not enough."

"Hey." Vito pretends to be hurt. "I'm not a little animal. I'm full-sized."

I tuck my forehead against the stubble growing along his neck. "Some things about you are definitely full-sized." I lower my hand to cup his butt cheek through his PJs. "And this too." I slide a hand between us to stroke his growing erection.

He groans, deep and low in his throat. "Baby," he hisses. "You're getting me excited in a whole different kind of way."

"Is that a bad thing?" I ask, pressing my fingertips lightly along the front of the drawstring and lower. His cock responds to my closeness. I press my full breasts against his bare chest and reach back around to grab his ass.

"Fuck," he sighs. "This is reason enough to go back to bed. You with me?"

"First one upstairs has to get the condom," I tell him.

"Has to?" He turns and faces me, then he playfully shoves me away from him, turning and dashing through the house, headed for the stairs.

I laugh and follow after him, keeping my footsteps light so we don't wake the baby. Nothing blocks grown-up time like a toddler awake before dawn.

By the time I get upstairs, Vito is sitting on the bed, his pajama pants off and a foil square tucked between two fingers. He's grinning like he's won a race.

"You're so competitive," I tease, turning so he can see my ass as I shimmy out of my bottoms. He sucks in a breath as I bend deep, step out of the sleepwear, and then turn back to face him.

"I've got three siblings," he says. "It's in my blood."

I smirk as I turn around and let him watch as I ease my super loose top over my shoulders. "I was an only child," I remind him. "I'm okay letting you win."

"Silly woman," he breathes. "You're the prize."

He watches me, his eyes dark and his lips parted as I climb onto the bed. I straddle his legs and climb all the way up his body until I'm just above his cock. I settle lightly against his erection, letting the heat of my pussy press into his length.

He sucks in a deep breath and closes his eyes, but

then he drops the condom on the sheet so he can hold my breasts in his hands. "These," he groans. "I could lose myself in them."

He holds the weight of me in his hands and squeezes lightly. The gentle pressure sends waves of desire through my body, my pussy growing even wetter in anticipation.

"More," I tell him, grabbing hold of his shoulders. I reach for the condom and tear it open, but just before I slide the latex over his flesh, I climb off his lap and kneel over his cock. "Touch me," I tell him as I open my mouth and flick my tongue over the head of his dick.

He growls deep in his chest, muttering thankful curses as I take him all the way into my mouth, lapping my tongue against him to make sure he's nice and wet before I roll on the condom.

He caresses my breasts softly as I suck him, until finally he's humming, and I know if I want to keep things going, I'm going to need to sheathe him up.

Once he's wearing the condom, I climb back over him and roll my hips back and forth along his length. He's not even inside me yet, but our pace is frantic and fast. I feel the thick muscles and soft hairs of his thighs between my legs, and I have to grip his shoulders for support.

He pinches my nipples in his fingertips, and I am close to losing it. I nearly cry out, the pleasure is so, so good. But then I lean forward and practically feed him my nipple.

He sucks the tip deep between his lips, the pleasure radiating through my chest and limbs. I am lost to the sweet, golden heat when he removes my nipple from his mouth and rolls his neck in circles while pressing my tender nipple against the stubble of his chin. I chase the ecstasy, rocking my hips against him while I throw my head back and let him work his magic.

I don't know how he does it because my eyes are slammed shut, but I feel him shove a hand between us. I lift my weight a little, but goddamn, my legs are so weak I can hardly support my weight. Then he shifts his erection, and I slide all the way down, crying out for real as his length reaches deep inside me.

"Fuck, I love you. I love this. I love you more, but fuck," he groans.

I can't speak. I'm lost to the colors swirling behind my eyes, to the burn in my thighs as I grind deeper, pressing my weight so every roll of my hips brings wave after wave of bliss through my body.

Once I slow my movements, sweat misting along

my hairline, Vito lifts me off his cock and lays me on my back.

He immediately grabs my thighs in his hands and spreads me wide.

I'm boneless, opening to him so he can see, touch, and taste every inch of my most private parts. He drops his mouth to my pussy.

"Fuck, you taste good," he grits out when he stops to suck in a chest full of air. "You have the sweetest pussy."

He pulls his mouth back and trails his fingertips along the insides of my thighs. He nibbles and kisses his way from my pubic bone to my right knee, then turns to pay the same attention to my left leg. I'm completely naked, my tits sagging on either side of my chest, my hair sweaty and matted against the sheets, and yet with his hands on my body, I feel like the most beautiful woman alive.

I curl my toes and try to sit up, but Vito shakes his head and massages the tight muscles in my legs. "I want to devour you," he says, pressing my legs open wider. He situates himself between my open legs and nudges my opening with his cock, murmuring, "You're the most gorgeous fucking woman alive."

I open my eyes a crack and smile at him, but then

I immediately slam my lids shut when Vito thrusts inside me.

I try to relax my legs and take the full pressure of every deep thrust inside me, but he's grabbing my legs and closing them together like a clothespin in front of his chest. I try to hold up the weight of my legs, but Vito's cock all the way inside me while my legs are together, my feet in the air, it's more than I can take. I cry out his name as yet another climax steals the strength from my limbs.

He patiently waits until my fingers loosen from the sheets to flip me onto my belly. I lift my butt in the air, but I can't even control my hands and legs. I need Vito to help lift my hips so he can fuck me from behind.

He slaps the side of my ass, the slap so loud I worry it will wake up Juniper, but honestly, it's worth it. When he finishes, he collapses on top of me, our sweaty bodies sticking together.

"That was freaking…" I can't even finish the thought. I squint at the clock and see that we have plenty of time to go back to sleep. The coffeepot has a four-hour safety shut-off, so I don't have to do anything or worry about anything until Juniper is awake.

I think Vito is thinking the same thing because

with a numb little grunt, he jerks the sheets up off the bed and tucks them in around us. He settles himself halfway on top of me, his face smashed against my right breast, while his leg is thrown over my right thigh.

"Love you," he says. "Sorry if I drooled on you a little just then."

I laugh as much as I can pinned beneath his weight, and I snake my fingers through his hair. "Love you," I whisper.

My mind is at ease. My heart is happy. If I thought buying this house was a dream come true, I know now that home ownership doesn't even come close to what I feel when I'm with this man.

This competitive, silly, real, firefighting Bianchi. I fall asleep with a smile on my face and the man I love literally on my heart.

"Holy fucking..." Gracie Bianchi—now Cooper—wanders through my new house with her son Ethan on her hip and her mouth wide open. She lifts a perfectly arched black brow at me. "Babe, when you said you bought a house, I was expecting a starter home.

This?" She sweeps her hand around the wide-open living room.

My head is spinning right now. Gracie offered to watch Juniper while I go in for my first day of orientation, and I have barely had enough coffee.

Vito has been on the last two nights, so I haven't slept well. That's becoming a real thing now that I know he plans to move in. But since he hasn't told his parents yet, I can't spill the news to Gracie.

"Hey." Gracie's voice is soft as she sets Ethan down on the playmat. He's just about Junie's age, and he immediately waddles, then drops to a crawl to take a toy from Junie's hand.

"Eden?" Gracie waves a heavily tattooed hand in my face. "Hey, girl. You look like you want to start crying. You know Junie's going to be just fine with me and Ethan, right?"

I nod and swallow hard against the emotions. "Yeah, of course. I'm really happy you're here. Thank you for agreeing to watch her."

"It's a lot, though. Going back to work." She nods at Ethan's dark brown ringlets of hair. "You got any coffee going?"

I shake my head. "I was up early and finished a pot. I haven't been sleeping."

Gracie nods, her long black hair grazing her

shoulders. Somehow, she looks effortlessly cool in an oversized, shredded concert T-shirt with a tank top underneath it and black jeans. She took her shoes off at the door, of course, and is barefoot. Even her black toenail polish looks perfect.

"How do you do it?" I ask. I drop down onto the floor beside the kids and cross my legs. "I don't think I've painted my toenails since before I got pregnant."

Gracie looks at me, her beautiful eyes rimmed with thick, winged liner. "Girl, I have Ryder. I couldn't do it without him."

I peek at the time on my watch and reassure myself I'm okay. It's only nine, and Michelle said I could stop by this morning for the hiring paperwork and a basic orientation. I figure a few minutes with Gracie is time well spent, because I have no one else in my life I can ask pressing questions. "Was postpartum hard for you?"

Gracie widens her eyes and shakes her head dramatically. "I was still adjusting to being a stepmom to two fully formed humans when this one came along." She jerks a thumb at her son. "I had some infertility issues before I conceived, and I thought the hardest part of all of this was going to be getting pregnant." She plops down on the floor beside me and tucks her feet under her butt.

"It wasn't?" I ask.

"Hell no." She picks at an invisible thread on her tee and shrugs. "I have a big personality." She flicks me a glance as if ready to fight me over the statement, but I just grin. "Ryder gave up his stable job teaching just before Ethan was born. He went to work for a start-up with his best friend, so he was putting in long hours. He cut back once the baby was born, of course, but I fell into a funk for sure. I'm not the kind of person who gets sad, though. I mean, I feel the feelings, but I tend to either go quiet or I get angry. You can probably guess how hard it was to be quiet with a newborn, two children, and a husband who was pulled in twenty directions."

I listen to her experience and can't imagine. I know how hard it was to do everything myself, but to multiply the responsibilities, to have a partner who was out of his routine, and to battle postpartum depression? I reach out a hand and squeeze her shoulder. "Gracie," I say. "How did you manage?"

She chuckles. "I drew a lot. In fact, that's one of the things that got me through. I leaned in to the one thing that has always been there for me. My art. I would swaddle the baby against my chest and sit the older kids down, and we would make art for hours." She waves a hand. "I wish our house was this big because, let me tell you, two kids and a professional tattoo artist can make a big old mess."

It dawns on me then that Gracie has this huge family. Where were they when she was going through all of this? "I'm surprised your mom wasn't constantly helping," I say, hoping I chose the right words.

"Girl, I had to kick my mother to the curb constantly. She'd have raised those kids if I'd let her." She lifts a perfect brow at me and points right at my chest. "You need to set boundaries with Lucia, because I'm telling you. Ma is all heart, and she's eyeballs-deep in good intentions, but she has no filter sometimes. So, if she's showing up day after day, offering to help, you take what you need. I love them to the moon and back. But I've been worried they've been making things too easy on my brother."

She grows quiet and looks at me.

"I'm about to spill some tea, so I sure hope you two are serious."

I smile and nod, but I don't say anything more. I don't want to speak behind Vito's back, but at the same time, I want to get to know Gracie better.

"So, here's the deal about my brother. Ah, crap." Gracie wrinkles her nose and leans in to sniff

Juniper's butt. "Not yours," she says. "That means it's mine."

She jumps up and grabs her diaper bag, which looks more like a giant metallic-gray purse than a diaper bag. "You mind if I do this here?" she asks. "Or do you prefer the bathroom?"

"Wherever you want."

She nods and pulls out a changing pad and bribes Ethan to stop playing by giving him a new toy. "I'll just say this," she says. "Divorce does funny things to some people, and Vito's did a number on him. He's spent five years of his adult life living with our parents. Don't get me wrong. After I went through some shit, I moved back in with Lucia and Mario too. But he's been there five years, and if you ask me, he's let himself get too comfortable. Maybe he's comfortable staying in the nest because he has no idea what direction to go if he tries to fly on his own."

Gracie stands Ethan up and lets him go play with Juniper. She's wadded up the diaper and wiped down the changing pad. "Where do you want this?"

I show her the way and then stay with the kids while she heads back into the powder room to wash her hands. When she comes back, she points to her wrist. She doesn't wear a watch, but I do, and I check the time.

"You probably need to get dressed?" she asks.

I nod, reluctant to get up. I could spend the whole day here with Gracie, Ethan, and Juniper.

Maybe Vito and I aren't that different. I'm not sure I want to leave my nest now that it's time to go.

"Nervous?" Gracie asks. "Going back to work after being home with these sweet cheeks all day is tough," she says. "But give Michelle a try. It's bananas thinking that she's now a financial adviser, but…" Gracie shrugs. "She was always good people. Vito is good people." She grins at me, her thick red lipstick perfectly coating her full lips. "You're good people. And it's never too late to try something new, you know?"

I give her a smile and make sure she knows where to find everything. I tell Gracie to make herself completely at home and show her how to turn on the television.

"All I care about is getting out in the yard," she says. "Come on, kiddos. Let's get sweaters. We're going to tire out some toddlers."

I head upstairs to take a quick shower, all thoughts of making another pot of coffee long gone. I'm sure if she wants it, Gracie will help herself. After all, she's practically family. And I intend to start treating her like it.

CHAPTER 17
VITO

THE LAST THREE days of my life have been like so many others over the years. You'd think every one of the horrible accidents or fires might be some of the worst or hardest shit I'd ever been through—until the next one.

I'm fortunate, working in a small town. We have a lot less of this stuff than bigger cities. This stuff being the calls that you feel under your skin. The sounds that lock in your ears and you don't know how you'll ever stop hearing them.

And yet, time passes.

The intensity of whatever the shit was eases. A little. Then a little more. Sometimes I wake up with my heart racing after a nightmare that brings just one small detail back, and that triggers a whole lot of memories. Emotions.

But still, this is the job. I may not like what it does to me, but I love what I do on calls like the ones we had this shift. It takes guts and teamwork to survive the day. It takes training, experience, and maturity to survive the aftermath.

When you get so close to other people's worst moments, worst days, it steals a little of the light from yours.

That's the trade-off.

When you hold the hand of the dying, you willingly give up a little part of the wholeness that makes you alive.

I did that and more today. And I'm fucking ready to go home and let the long, slow process of dealing with it all start.

My shift is over, and I've changed and showered. The mood is intense. The silence among the guys in my engine company is as overpowering and dense as smoke.

I grab my bag and keys and stand on shaky knees, ready to haul ass out of there, when Chief joins us.

His eyes carry the weight of what we're all feeling. I know he's been filling out a ton of paperwork and working on scheduling a critical incident debriefing. That means he's not able to pack what we saw into a tiny box until the intensity fades like the sun hiding behind a cloud. He's had to stare right into that blinding light for longer than any of us.

"Tomorrow," Chief says quietly. No one needs to ask what he means. "Three p.m. sharp. I'm trying to get someone out from Columbus to do a second session for anyone who needs it. This is mandatory."

I nod and brush past the chief, ready to get the fuck out of here. The chief stops me with a hand on my shoulder. "Good work today. Leadership like that made a difference."

"Thanks." The words feel like wool in my mouth. None of what I did today made a bit of difference to the outcome.

I did my best. We all did.

I get out to my truck, and fresh morning air hits my face. I breathe it in, the smells of the call we finished overnight still thick in my nose. I shake my head.

There's no residue. I followed all the protocols. Wore all the gear. Washed away any traces of what happened, but there are some stains that never, ever go away.

This is the part of the job that isn't glamorous. That isn't fun.

These are the things I lock away inside myself when I go home and sleep.

It's just after seven, and I need to sleep. It's only Eden's third day on the job, and as far as I can remember, Sassy's watching Juniper. My mind goes to shit after a shift like that. It takes some time before I can pull myself from the intensity of the work and get back to the routine of life outside the station.

Once I'm inside my truck, I slam the door hard, images from the night playing like a movie in my mind. I close my eyes against the memories, but that only makes them easier to see.

I check my phone, and there's a photo message from Eden waiting on my phone. It's only a picture of her legs. She's sitting on her bed, her legs crossed. She's wearing a black pencil skirt, black nylons, and sexy high heels.

Eden: Missed u, babe. Missed u bad. This will be waiting for you when you get to my place. Can't wait for you to move in.

I'm supposed to go to Eden's this afternoon after she's off work and after I get some decent sleep. But I can't think that far into the future. I can't reply to her text. I can't do anything but think about what I saw, and I want to stop thinking about it.

I'll be back here tomorrow for the meeting with

the therapist, and we'll all go back over it. It's usually the same one, somebody the chief calls in from another county.

It often helps if the person is a total outsider. If the therapist knows the people involved in the traumatic incident, the one that was so bad a whole crew of experienced first responders needed stress debriefing, that makes the whole process a lot tougher.

Some of the therapists are better than others. Most invite us to talk but let us stay silent if that's how we need to deal. Intervening early and giving us the chance to get what happened off our chests is supposed to lead to less PTSD, fewer guys like me having real problems because we can't deal with the stress.

I toss my phone onto the passenger seat and crank the music up full blast. My ears are ringing by the time I pull into the driveway at my parents'.

I walk in the front door, a fucking grimace on my face that's so heavy, my jaw literally hurts. I kick off my shoes and head into the kitchen just in time to see my father with his hand under my mother's robe.

"Jesus Fucking Christ!" I shout and stagger back. Thankfully, Pops is fully dressed, but he sure as hell was getting a handful of something.

"Vito." Ma clutches her robe closed at the top.

Her hair and makeup are not done, and I'm shocked to see her not dressed at this hour. "We thought you were going to text us if you were coming back. We assumed you were going to crash at Eden's."

"Plans changed," I grumble, but then I drop my phone on the counter and brace myself on my palms.

"Oh shit." Pops comes around the counter and claps a hand on my shoulder. "What happened, son? Is it Eden?"

I whip my head up, and my heart practically parkours its way out of my chest. "No." I shake my head. "Multiple fatalities. It was bad."

Ma immediately runs to the sink and starts a kettle for tea. Pops is quiet, but his hand on my shoulder is firm. "When's the debrief?" he asks, his voice low.

"Tomorrow," I say. "Three."

Ma gets a mug and drops a tea bag into it, then scurries around gathering fruit and bread for toast while the kettle boils. "Just something light to eat, baby," she says.

I nod. This is the routine. This is what it's like supporting a guy like me with a job like this. This is the shit my siblings don't see.

They may think I live with our parents because I'm lazy or directionless. I stay because they are my safe place to land. Always have been.

"Ma," I say. "Can you put that tea in a to-go cup? I'm going to grab some fresh clothes and head out."

Ma looks to my pops, tears filling her eyes. "You want me to drive you? You look so tired, son."

I never like this part, but it's always a component of the routine. I lie. Not a big lie, but one that will keep the pain that could tear me apart under control, so that it doesn't shatter the hearts of the people I love.

"Ma," I grumble, trying desperately to find some humor but coming up with very little. "Don't pretend you and Pops won't get right back to what you were doing when I walked in the second I'm out that door." I give her a weak smile. "I'm all right."

She packs up some fruit and hands me the toast on a paper plate. "Eat this before it gets cold. I'll have the rest ready when you come down." She comes around the counter and slips her arms around my waist. She hugs me hard, her soft body going tight. The strength of my tiny mother, the way she's trying to hug the hurt right out of me... It makes my eyes burn and my nose prickle.

"All right," I say, blinking fast and stepping out of her hold. "Thanks, Ma."

I head upstairs and throw clothes and toiletries into a gym bag. I don't think, just grab and shove, until I realize I need socks and underwear, and I grab those too. I head back downstairs, where Ma has a massive casserole carrier waiting for me.

"I'm sending some leftovers, so you just have to heat up lunch." Ma shoves the bag of food at me. "You come home tonight or tomorrow if you need us, baby."

Her eyes are red, but she's not crying. Pops grabs the food from Ma and says, "I'll walk you to your truck."

I don't argue but stop to kiss my mother goodbye before heading to the door, putting on my shoes, and grabbing my keys. Pops is right on my heels, and he goes around the passenger side to put the food on the seat next to my gym bag.

Then he comes around to the driver's side. "This is always your home. You don't need to call."

I nod. "Tell Ma to stock up on bleach," I say, managing a grin. "If I see any more than what I did today, I'm going to need to bleach my eyes."

Pops lightly slaps my chest with the back of his hand, then tugs me close for a hug. He watches from the driveway, and I see Ma standing at the door holding the front of her robe closed, waving as I drive away.

I turn the tunes back on, drown out my thoughts and worries, and focus on driving.

I'm almost home.

When I get to Eden's, Shirley's car is gone, and the house looks empty. I shoot Sassy a text to see what's up, and she replies back with two messages—one text and a picture.

Sassy: Took Junie to the park. Be back later.

I realize as soon as I let myself into the quiet house how much I was hoping to see Juniper. Somehow seeing her innocent, sweet face and dropping down to play with blocks or a playset would do my heart some good.

Since Juniper's at the park and Eden is at work, I shoot a text back to Sassy.

Me: I let myself in, Sass. I'm at Eden's house. Going to catch some sleep till you're back.

I put the leftovers from Ma away in the kitchen and head upstairs to Eden's bedroom and change from my jeans into pajama pants and a T-shirt. I climb under the covers and take a picture of my face against her pillows and shoot off a quick text to Eden.

Me: Rough call at work. I came here instead of

my parents'. I needed to be close to you, even if you're not here. Love you. Have a good day, babe.

I click send on both the text and the picture, then I get up and close the door and draw the curtains. It's still really bright in here, so I grab a blanket from the foot of the bed and hang it over the curtain rod to dampen more of the daylight.

Once it's dark and quiet, I climb under the covers and put a pillow over my head. I block out all the light and sound and just breathe. I say a prayer for the people whose lives were lost last night. For the guys on my crew. For everyone I love. I breathe deep and catch the light fragrance of Eden's shampoo. The scent of her hair. The familiar smells comfort me, and I close my eyes. Before I know it, I give in to dream-less sleep.

When I wake up, I know immediately that I'm not in my small bed back at my parents'. The super-soft sheets and comforter remind me that even though I can't see for shit, I'm at Eden's.

I toss back the blankets and stumble into the attached bathroom. When I click on the light, I see how puffy my eyes are. I splash some cold water on my face and brush my teeth because my mouth feels like a wasteland.

I see a pencil skirt, a pair of hose, and a white blouse neatly resting on the side of the bathtub, which means Eden must have come home and changed, and I didn't hear a thing.

I'm still in pajamas, but I don't bother changing.

I check my phone and see that it's after six. I have messages from my parents, two from Franco, and even one from Benito.

Word travels fast through the Bianchi family. Ma must have told them I had a rough day.

I don't, however, have any messages from Eden.

I wiggle my toes into my house slippers and head toward the stairs. When I reach the landing, I see Eden holding Juniper. They are swaying in front of the television, which is on at a very low volume. I can hear Eden and Junie quietly singing along with an animated kids movie.

I just stand there for a minute watching them.

Eden's long, soft hair sweeps her back as she sways. She kisses Junie's cheeks as they watch the show and sing. I can't believe how quiet the volume is, but I'm sure they don't need to hear it to know the words.

Watching them like this, I am overcome by the

need to rush down the stairs. To crush them in my arms and keep them close. I want them in my home, in my arms, and in my heart always.

I was right to come here instead of staying at my parents'.

This is where I belong.

This is my family.

My home.

I walk down the stairs, calling out softly so I don't scare the shit out of them. "You didn't have to stay quiet for my sake."

Eden turns, and Juniper squeals out, "Veelo. Veelo."

Eden laughs and repeats after her daughter. "Veelo."

They meet me at the bottom of the stairs. Eden studies my face. She looks so happy to see me.

"You're the most beautiful thing I've ever seen," I tell her.

Her eyes mist, and she grins. "You just want to get some later," she teases.

"Did it work?" I ask.

She waggles her brows at me and moves Junie to one arm, stepping close to fold the three of us together in an awkward family hug. I clutch her tightly and smooch Junie loudly on the cheek.

"You must be starving," she says. "We waited to have dinner."

"You did?" I ask.

She nods. "Come on." She passes Juniper to me, and I cuddle the soft, happy, wiggling thing in my arms.

"How was the park, Juniper? Did Auntie Sassy take you on the swings?"

Juniper starts babbling, and I try to follow her very excited syllables while we walk behind Eden into the kitchen. She pulls Juniper's kiddie seat up to the table, but when I try to put her in her chair, she tightens her arms around my neck. I swap a look with Eden, and she nods, a huge smile on her face.

Since the little nugget seems to want to stay with me, I sit down in the eating nook and settle her on my lap. She's drooling, and a little puddle of spit falls on her chin. I wipe it with my thumb and then wipe the drool on my pajama pants.

The agony of my shift hovers like a shadow behind my back, but my back is strong. Stronger now with my family around me. I'm okay. And I'm going to be okay. Because tonight is just another night.

We're going to eat my parents' leftovers. Put this perfect baby to bed. And then I'm going to ask about Eden's day. Listen to the stories of her new job. I won't share what happened because I want to protect her in every way I can. Even from the demons that chase me down. But that's okay. Because together, we are safe. Together, we are strong enough to weather the job stresses. The money worries. The tears and the laughs. Together, we are home.

CHAPTER 18
EDEN

I FUCKED UP, and I mean I fucked up bad.

The last month of my new job has been a blur. I have so many passwords for so many systems, I spend half my time searching for my notes and trying to remember how to do the thousand little things that come up in a day. Gennie must have been the world's most patient person because almost every morning, I wake up with a sick feeling in the pit of my stomach just thinking about the notes I've taken to try to remember how to do everything.

It's not getting any easier. In fact, it's getting worse.

Every morning for the last four weeks, I've had to drag myself out of bed and remind myself that it's normal to be completely lost at a new job.

It's completely normal to have to ask a thousand questions.

It's completely normal to feel like a failure from the moment I pull into the parking lot until the moment I pull back out at the end of my workday.

As far as employers go, Michelle has been great. Friendly, positive, patient. She's strict, though, and I can sense her losing patience with me as the days creep by.

The other day, I was technically not on a lunch break but was so desperate not to feel stupid for five minutes, I started reading a book on my phone. Of course, that was the exact time that Michelle walked out and caught me reading. She was not happy, and she asked if I had spare time, if I would please ring her so she could train me on some other aspect of the business.

I felt ashamed. I mean, I've had jobs before. Lots of them. I started working the second I could get a work permit at fifteen. I know better than to slack off while I'm on the clock, but this is nothing like what I expected.

I'm learning nothing about money and finances but a lot about running a small office, how many software systems it takes to run a small business, and how intimate it is working day-today with only a handful of people around to ask for help.

When Michelle asks me for something, I feel this intensity, like she's counting the seconds until I get the job done. It's not like she's mean or pressuring me; it's just how she runs her company. She's good at what she does. She talks to a lot of people, makes a lot of calls. Is hands on with everything. Which really sucks when you're the person who seems not to know how to do anything.

And then, I made a mistake.

A big, big mistake.

I know it's only been a month, but the very first day I started, Gennie trained me on the small stuff. Using the calendar system so Michelle always knows when she has in-office appointments. How to take messages so nothing ever gets lost. Don't even ask me how many times I got locked out of my voice mail because I punched in the wrong password.

Yesterday was incredibly busy. A call came in from a very wealthy client. I still think of all the clients as rich people. No matter how many times Michelle tries to tell me to use one of the more delicate phrases—high-net-worth individuals or some such—they are all just rich people to me.

So, a guy in town who owns like three commercial properties wanted to ask Michelle if she could get him a better rate on something than what he was about to get from his current adviser.

He said he hated to rush her, but he was going out of town and wanted to make a quick decision. I honestly didn't understand half of what he said.

All I do know is that he said he hoped Michelle would call him right back. I let him know she was in a meeting in her office with an appointment, took his information, and uploaded the details to the system.

I didn't think about it again until five minutes ago when I got to my desk and found Michelle waiting for me, her lips an unusually angry line.

"Eden," she says. "Do you remember putting Randall Tomlinson into the system yesterday?"

No good morning. No how are you. She hits me with this question, and the only thing I can think of when she says Tomlinson is a guy from a very famous boy band. I put like three new people into the system yesterday, but I don't know which one she's referring to.

"I think so," I say, already starting to sweat. "Did I do something wrong, Michelle?"

She sighs and shakes her head. "You tell me." She nods toward the computer on my desk and stands over me while I rack my brain to try to think of who this guy is and why she's making a big show of asking me about him.

My fingers are shaking as I try to log in, but Michelle groans and waves me away. "Let me," she says.

I literally get up out of my chair and stand over her as she sits at my desk, taps a million miles an hour at the keyboard, and pulls up a screen on the system I swear I've never seen.

"Look here," she says, pointing at the monitor with a finger. "This morning, I ran a report of all the new entries in the database. Three new contacts were entered yesterday." She points to one name and shows me a field where the other financial adviser, Glenn, made contact with the client and made a bunch of notes about the plan of action.

"I see," I say quietly because I do see it, but I don't understand what I'm looking at.

"And this one." Michelle sounds just plain tired now. "See this note here?"

I bend a little closer and see that Michelle herself put in a note this morning disqualifying the person because of a pending bankruptcy.

"Yes, that lead is unqualified," I say, hoping like hell I've used the right words.

"And what's missing here?" she asks. She opens the client data screen for this Tomlinson person.

"Nothing?" I ask. "No adviser assessment or contact was made?"

She slams a hand down on the desk. "Yes. Do you know why that is?" she asks.

I'm starting to get really sick of this game. "Michelle, please don't treat me like I'm stupid," I say. "If I made a mistake, please just say it. Show me what I did, and I'll make notes about what you want so I can try not to do it again."

I can't keep the irritation from my voice. This job sucks. I've been feeling it and thinking it. It's not Michelle. It's the whole business. I want to understand how to manage my money. I don't want to put a million transactions into a million systems and get called on the carpet like I'm an idiot. Maybe I am an idiot. Maybe I just don't care enough. Whatever it is, I'm starting to believe this job—this field, even—is not for me.

"Eden," Michelle says, her voice taking on a cold note that I've never heard before. "I have a history with Vito, and I thought—"

"Oh no." I hold up a finger. "Do not bring Vito into this. He has nothing to do with my performance on this job. If I've fucked up, you make this talk we're having about the work. This has nothing to do with my relationship or your ex."

Michelle is quiet, and she runs her tongue over her teeth, seeming to think for a minute. "This is my place of business, and I'd appreciate if you'd let me finish my statement."

I can't help myself. I cross my arms over my chest and lift my brow. "Please," I say, "finish your thought. What exactly did I do wrong?"

She sighs and waves her hand toward the computer. "You neglected to assign the contact to me, Eden. That means that Tomlinson is stuck in the system without a contact owner." Everything else she says is a blur of buzzwords and jargon that I don't think I could repeat if my life depended on it. What I guess from her gesturing and tone is that I didn't pass along the message the right way.

"Wait," I say. "So, he's the guy who wanted the call back about the competing rate?"

Michelle's tone is condescending as she says, "You do remember. So, what? Is this all an act, then? I'm so flustered, I can't remember my own password."

My mouth falls open. "Are you mocking me?"

Michelle backpedals immediately. "I'm sorry. That was inappropriate. But you have to understand mistakes like this, carelessness about the tiniest details, those are the kinds of things that cost me money, Eden. Clients at this level expect a certain type of professionalism and service. You're just not meeting the expectations I had for you."

I'm not meeting expectations... I don't need a finance degree to know what that means.

"I'm not working out here," I say, not waiting for her to agree. "You took a chance on me, and I'm not good enough. Say no more."

"Eden, wait." Michelle leans her butt against the side of my desk. "I thought I could do something good for you, make up to Vito all the shit I put him through in the past. I still think you can learn this stuff. You just have to try harder. Pay attention. Care more. You have to act as though every client's business means the difference between making money and losing face."

I shake my head. "No," I say. "Michelle, I don't know why you thought offering me a job was a good idea. If you have shit to work out with Vito, see a shrink. He's moved on, and this..." I wave my hand around. "I don't need these kinds of favors from anyone." Since I haven't even put my purse down, I don't have to do anything but turn and march out of there. I start to, but then I turn back.

"Michelle," I say, "I looked up to you. I looked forward to learning from someone whom I thought saw something in me. But you've treated me just like you treated Vito. You want me to be better, faster, more than I am. You could have been more patient, but that would have just convinced me I should try harder at something that I already know isn't right for me." I clutch my purse and nod at her. "Thank you for the opportunity. I have learned a lot in the time I've worked for you, and I sincerely do appreciate that. I wish you all the best."

I turn on my heel and don't wait for her to fire me before I walk out.

It's still early. Today, Sassy and Lucia took Juniper and Ethan over to a massive sports complex that Gracie's husband Ryder manages.

Before I even realize what's happening, I'm heading to downtown Star Falls. It's not even noon yet, but sometimes Gracie goes to her sister-in-law's bookstore for coffee and peanut butter crisps before she starts work.

I park my car outside the bookstore and head inside. Chloe is at the front desk, tapping away at something on her iPad.

"Eden?" She comes around the counter and gives me a huge hug. I haven't spent a ton of time with

Chloe over the last few months. Since she owns the bookstore, she doesn't come to Lucia's brunches, but she is a fixture at Sunday night family dinners.

I'm not as close to her as I am to Gracie, but I hope that can change in time.

"Hey, Chloe." I give her a weak hug and then sigh. "Any chance you have a book that can help me decide what to be when I grow up?"

"Oh God." She motions toward the back of the shop. "This sounds like a coffee and treat situation. You have time?"

I nod. "Nothing but time."

She runs to the back to grab some coffee, and I stroll through the children's book aisle and pick up a book for Junie, and then I wander back to the counter and pay for it.

"So…" Chloe pushes a coffee and a peanut butter crisp toward me.

"Mmm," I purr over the yummy treat. "These are amazing. I'd love to learn how to bake if you're willing to teach me someday," I tell her. "You don't have to give away your recipe for these, but I'd love to learn to bake anything. I'm pretty basic in the kitchen."

Chloe nods. "Of course. I have some great cookbooks, too, I can loan you if you like to read. I don't keep a huge stock on hand in the store because so many people now are finding their recipe inspirations online. But I'll bring some to Sunday dinner for you."

When she says that, my throat goes a little bit dry and it's not from the cookie. She says it—she'll bring me something when she sees me at the next family dinner, like it's the most normal thing in the world.

Since when did having things like family dinners become so normal to me?

I feel like so much about my life is changing so fast, and instead of being scared or resisting it, I'm just happy. At least, with my home life and family, that is.

"What's this about needing help with what you want to be when you grow up?"

I sigh. "I don't know. I want to have a job that I love. Work that matters, you know? How did you know you wanted to do this?"

An elderly lady wearing a pair of bright-red-framed eyeglasses comes in and goes right up to the counter. She greets me in a very loud voice, and her colorful clothes make me think of Lucia's lady gang. The woman has perfectly styled white hair, and though she's pretty tiny and bent over, she's got a lot of spunk.

"Sorry to barge in." She sets a hand knotted by

age on the counter, her nails painted bright red just like her glasses. "Chloe, I'm on the hunt for a book, doll. What do you get for the man who has everything?"

"Rita, is this for another boyfriend?" Chloe covers her mouth. "What happened to Mad Max?"

The older lady, Rita, blows air between her lips. "There's old and there's *old*. And that man was old. I've upgraded to a younger model." She covers her mouth with a hand and stage-whispers, "He's twenty-two years younger."

Chloe cackles and then points to me. "Rita, have you met Eden yet?"

Rita swivels on her heel and gives me her full attention. Her sharp eyes take me in, and she points a finger at me. "I don't know you, doll." She sticks out her hand. "I'd remember a beautiful face like that. And wow, you're tall."

I take her hand in mine and shake it lightly. "Nice to meet you," I say.

Chloe explains that I'm dating Vito, and before she can get out another word, Rita gasps. "Well, of course. No wonder I haven't met you. Vito knows better than to bring a beautiful woman around his brother. Have you met Benito yet?"

I nod. "I have, many times. I see him when he stops by the Sunday family dinners."

Rita looks pissed. "So, you're telling me Vito has brought you to family dinners but not to Benito's restaurant."

"Rita is the hostess at Benito's place," Chloe explains.

I grin. That explains so much. Every woman over fifty connected to the Bianchis must be cut from the same cloth—colorful, loud, and loving.

Rita motions for me to bend closer, and I do. "Come see me over lunch service. I'll make sure you get the best seat in the house."

"It's kid-friendly," Chloe adds. Then she tells Rita, "Eden has a daughter. She's about the same age at Ethan."

Rita practically crows. "Other people's children are my favorite kind. Bring the little one," she says, then she's back to business. "I'm looking for something maybe romantic. A little naughty would be good, very naughty even better. What do you have?" she asks.

Chloe winks at me and leads Rita toward the back of the store just as the front door opens, and a very familiar face makes my heart jump.

"What the heck are you doing here?" I rush through the store to give him a huge hug.

He kisses me lightly on the lips. "Hey, gorgeous. I think the real question is, what are you doing here? Aren't you supposed to work today?"

Crap.

"Well," I say. "Yeah. I mean, I was at work. I think we should maybe talk about it at home."

Vito's gorgeous face looks grim. "Something happen? Did Michelle do something?" He motions around the store. "You done here? You want to take a walk?"

I nod. "Yeah, I paid for my stuff. Let me grab my book." Vito takes my coffee cup, while I slip Junie's book into my purse. "You want the last bite?" I ask, offering him the very tiny bit of peanut butter crisp that's left.

"That's how I know you love me," he says, pointing to his open mouth.

I feed him the last bite and toss the paper wrapper into the trash bin behind the counter. "Should we say bye to Chloe?" I ask.

He cups his mouth and shouts, "Bye, Chloe. We got to run."

I laugh and hear a soft, "Bye, guys," echo from the back of the store.

Outside, we hold hands, lacing our fingers together. We stroll down Main Street past the store-fronts, some open, some closed. The Body Shop, where Gracie works, is dark. She'll be here in an hour or so to open. It's wild to me that a place I'd never even visited six months ago is so familiar.

Star Falls has been close to perfect since the moment I drove into town, and it's only gotten better.

Most of it, at least.

I tighten my grip on Vito's hand and slow my steps a little. "Maybe we should talk about this at home. I..." I don't know where to start. I didn't even think about how Vito would react to what happened today.

"Babe." He stops completely in the middle of the sidewalk, stepping aside with a grin to let the people walking behind us pass. Once we're alone, he cups my face. "We can go home, but you've got me worried as fuck. What happened?"

"It's nothing bad," I say.

He relaxes his hold on my cheeks and nods. "Okay. You want to start talking?"

I shrug. "I think I got fired today. But I'm not sure because I kind of told Michelle off and left."

Vito's eyes widen, and he's silent for a second. "Okay," he finally says. "You want to back up? What the hell happened?" I can see the wheels beginning to move behind his eyes, and he's starting to look pissed.

I shake my head. "I don't like the job. I thought I would. I thought I'd like finance, but running a small office is the worst. I made a mistake, and Michelle got a little shitty with me—"

He clenches his hands into fists, and I stop him with a hand on his shoulder.

"She threw some weird shit about you at me, and I just lost it. It was polite enough, but I think it's clear that job wasn't going to work out."

"What do you need me to do?" he asks, shoving his hands into his pockets. "I don't know what to feel here, Eden."

"Babe." I touch the scruff on his chin, the beautiful, prickly stubble that sends little ripples of excitement through my body just touching him like this, out on the sidewalk in front of the world. "Can we please go home? I want to think through what to do, and I just..." I check the time on my phone. "Your mom has got Juniper at Ryder's gym thing with Ethan and Sassy."

His expression is grim, and I honestly don't know whether he's mad at me or with me. But it's better I find out now while there may still be time to fix it.

CHAPTER 19
VITO

I'M glad I have the drive home to myself to sort out my feelings. The first thing I feel is rage.

If Michelle made Eden feel any kind of way—bad about herself, bad about me—I'm going to march my ass into that office and tear her a new one. Ex-wife or not, she has no right to talk shit to Eden.

I trusted that Michelle was more mature than that. I trusted that her intentions toward Eden were honest. Maybe I should be a lot less trusting and a lot more protective.

I won't make that mistake again.

"Tell me everything," I demand, pointing to the couch for Eden to sit. "Because if I need to go over there, I won't even take off my shoes."

"Vito," she says. She slips out of her high heels,

and together, we walk to sit side by side on the couch. "Are you mad at her or me?"

I can't help the look on my face. I'm sure I'm looking at her like she grew horns, but I can't imagine on what planet she'd think I'm mad at her. "I don't care if you took a shit on her office floor," I tell her. "I'd never be mad at you." I curl the side of my mouth in a grin. "I might offer to rent a carpet cleaner to help with the damage, but be mad at you? Babe, I trust you. I love you. Whatever happened, I'm on your side."

She shakes her head. "I fucked up. I missed a step putting in some data and might have cost Michelle a big client."

I frown. "That sucks, but so what? That's a pretty fragile business if some data-entry error can cost Michelle a client."

She nods, the long layers of her hair falling around her shoulders. "Michelle is pretty intense," she says. "She's great at what she does, but I didn't like it. It was passwords and lame shit that, honestly, I just didn't care about."

I nod. "Do you think it's just the newness of everything, or do you think you really don't like the field?"

She shrugs. "Both. I don't know. It wasn't the

right job for me. I'm sure about that. I just have no idea what else I'd want to do."

I blow air through my lips. "Put a pin in that. What the hell did Michelle say about me, and do I need to beat anyone's ass today? I wouldn't hit Michelle, but if I need to blast some eardrums, I'm ready to start yelling."

Eden shakes her head and looks down at her lap. "No, it was fine. It was. She said something about trying to make amends to you by helping me, but I told her I didn't want her bringing you into my job performance."

"Good on you," I tell her. "Anything else?"

"No. It wasn't that big of a deal, it just felt huge. I've never walked out on a job before."

I pull Eden close to me and smooth the hair back from her face. "That takes balls, baby. Not a lot of people would do that, no matter the circumstances." I take in the tightness around her lips and the sad way she's furrowing her brows. "So, you're unemployed? Are you worried?"

She sighs. "Yes, I'm unemployed again, I guess. And no, I'm not worried. I'm just bummed. What the hell do I do with my life now?"

"You try something new, babe. It's that simple.

And if you hate it, you move on to the next. Rinse and repeat."

"You make it sound so easy. Like it's no big deal. Did you ever think about doing anything else with your life? Do you ever think about the what-ifs?"

"I think about quitting almost every shift," I admit quietly. "When I see the kind of shit I see, I always wonder if that last call is going to be the one that breaks me. Make it so I can't go back, even if I want to."

She's stroking my thigh with a hand as I talk, and the effect is incredibly distracting but in the best way.

"But then I think about why I do it. And I know I'll never be able to sit back and hear sirens and not respond. It's just who I am. I'm sorry figuring out a career hasn't been that straightforward for you, but can I make a suggestion?"

"Anything," she says.

"Maybe steer clear of my exes. I think we can assume that shit won't end well."

She laughs and says, "Exes? What, do I need a list of names or something?"

"You've already worked for the big one, so I think you're pretty safe. Maybe don't apply for a job at the high school. Or the middle school…"

"Vito."

"I'm teasing," I tell her, although I did ghost a middle school teacher last summer and had to block her number, but that's not something we need to get into today.

"So, I guess I won't need to buy any more suits," she says, looking down at the pencil skirt and tailored blouse.

"Hmm," I mumble. "Or you could just buy them for me. I can think of a lot of ways to make sure your wardrobe doesn't go to waste."

"Like what?" she asks. "We've got some time before Juniper and your mom are due back here."

"Yes," I hiss and grab her hand. "It's like surprise date night in the middle of the day." I tug her up the stairs and close and lock the bedroom door behind us.

"This is like early Christmas," she breathes.

I nod, heat flooding my body. "And you are the sexiest package under the tree."

She rests her rear on the edge of the bed and crosses her legs. "So, you like my business attire?"

"I like it so much, I want to tear it off your body," I say, licking my lips. "I want to take off those hose with my teeth."

Eden giggles and lifts her brows at me. "I'm not sure how easy that's going to be with this skirt on. Maybe I should take that off first?"

I shake my head. "Let me do everything." I stand in front of her and reach for her hands so I can help her up off the bed. "Turn, please," I say, wrapping my hands around her waist and spinning her around so she's facing the bed.

She laughs again, her hair twirling and grazing my face with its luscious, vanilla-coconut scent as she turns. "Now what?"

I reach for the waistband of the skirt and feel for the hook closure at the back. I unfasten it, then grab the zipper, and, inch by slow inch, work my hand along the length of her ass. Once the zipper is undone, I put a hand on either side of her ass and massage her through the fabric of the unzipped skirt.

"Your body," I whisper, dropping to my knees. I reach for the skirt and work it slowly over her hips. I stop when the fabric is just past her butt and suck in a breath. "Do you not wear underwear to work?"

She looks at me over her shoulder, a playful expression on her face. "Maybe?"

"Oh God." In one swift move, I yank the skirt down around her ankles, revealing her long, thick legs wrapped in sheer black nylons. "Not going to lie," I say, running my hands over her ass. "I'm thinking about biting right through these."

Her whole body trembles lightly. "These are cheap drugstore hose."

"Noted." I shove her forward onto the bed. "Get comfortable," I tell her. "I'm going to take my time."

While she's lying facedown, I unbutton my jeans and shed my flannel. When I'm barefoot and in my boxers, I open her legs as wide as they will go while she's still facedown. Then I climb onto the bed behind her and kiss every inch of her left leg, starting at the calf.

I massage the soft fabric of the nylons under my hands as I blow hot kisses along her skin. She wriggles and moans while I work my way up to her thigh, but then I switch and cover her right leg in as much attention as I gave the left.

"Good?" I ask, landing a firm smack against her butt.

"Oh yes." She's resting with her left cheek on the bed, so I can see her eyes are closed and her mouth slightly open. "Babe, that is intense."

"Good." I knead the back of her thighs and calves through the hose until her breathing becomes so even, I'm afraid she's going to fall asleep. That is the opposite of what I want. I move up to her waist and push the hem of her blouse up so the waistband of her hose is exposed. Then I start kissing her lower back, flicking my tongue along her bare skin. She moans and wiggles her hips in response, so I add a little teeth.

I nip at her soft, hot skin and try to grab a bit of the fabric between my teeth, but I end up cracking up and giving in. "All right, I may need to take these off, not bite them off."

Eden lifts her head and says in a soft whisper, "I want them off."

A feral growl works its way from my chest to my lips. "Turn over."

She rolls onto her back and unbuttons her blouse, exposing the modest petal-pink bra underneath.

"Shirt off," I demand, and still lying back, she works her arms out of the sleeves. "Show me your gorgeous breasts."

She nudges the thin satin bra cups past her nipples, the erect peaks stiff and pink. My mouth waters to taste them, but first, I have plans for these hose.

I climb onto the bed and sit between her legs, reaching for the nylons. I make quick work of them and toss them to the floor before I settle my face between her thighs.

I turn my head and kiss her inner thigh, squeezing

her thick legs with my hands while working her tender skin with my mouth.

Her breathing is ragged and she's trying to bend her knees, but I use my palms to open her legs as wide as they can go.

I lower my mouth and suck hard, drawing her soft skin into my mouth.

I dip two fingers in my mouth to wet them, then make a V-shape with my fingers and stroke her outer lips.

"V," she breathes, clutching the comforter in her hands. "I need you inside me." And then she's gone before I can protest.

She hustles from the bed to the bathroom, opens and closes a drawer, and then comes back with a condom already out of the foil. She rolls it over my dick, then strokes my balls lightly with her nails.

"Eden…" I pant.

She smiles and straddles my legs and lowers herself onto my cock. We both moan as I enter her, the feeling as perfect and delicious as ever.

Arousal weakens my hands and knees, and I just lie there, my back against the pillows, while Eden grips my shoulders with her hands and grinds on my cock with long, sensual movements of her belly and hips.

I open my eyes to watch her, her chest flushed pink, her nipples still hard and exposed over the bra cups. I feel a tightening deep in my gut, and I can hardly keep my eyes open, the pleasure is so, so good. Eden's movements are sexy and slow until she whimpers and starts working her hips so fast and rhythmically, we're banging the bed frame against the wall.

But then, just as she arches her back and cries out, both of our phones ping at once with the distinctive chime of the home security system.

She clamps her lips closed and rides out her climax, then drops forward and whispers in my ear, "Hurry, babe. Fuck me hard."

She doesn't need to say another word of invitation. I grip her hips to hold her in place and pound into her as fast as I can. Within seconds, I'm falling over the edge and spilling inside the condom, my breathing rapid and my hair falling forward into my eyes.

"We need more of these afternoons," I grunt as she climbs off me, taking the condom with her.

"Let's not tell anyone I got fired. At least until we have one more morning to ourselves. Deal?"

I lean forward and grab her arm, pulling her back toward the bed so I can kiss her. "Deal, baby. Now, get rid of that, and let's get changed before my ma comes up here looking for us."

She giggles and hustles off to the bathroom. I grab my phone and send my ma a text, not at all willing to trust that she won't run up here to say hello since both our cars are outside.

Me: Remember the other day when I walked in on you and Pops in the kitchen? Unless you're in the mood for paybacks, keep Junie downstairs for about five more minutes.

I immediately get a text back with a load of smiley face and mind-blown emojis. I just grin because she's exactly right. That's exactly how I feel. And I have never, ever been happier.

EPILOGUE

EDEN

SIX MONTHS LATER

I TIGHTEN Juniper's scarf around her neck while I wait for Vito to unlock his parents' house. We're arriving a little later than planned, and I'm afraid we're going to miss seeing Benito before he has to get back to the restaurant.

Vito gives me a bright smile as he holds the door open, and I slosh through the front door in my snow boots. I take off little Junie's boots and jacket and set her on her feet. She's walking like crazy now, and she can't stand to be carried except through the ankle-deep snow.

As soon as she's down, she takes off running and squeals when she almost crashes into Ethan, who is lying on the floor playing with Lucia's older lab mix.

We decided to wait until summer to get a dog, when house-training won't mean constantly mopping up snow and slush from the floor. If the way Junie plays with her grandparents' dogs is any indication, she's going to absolutely adore having a puppy of her own in a few months.

Vito kicks off his boots and hangs both his coat and mine on hooks by the door while I unlace my boots.

"Benny?" Vito cocks his head at the full house ahead of us. "I thought we'd miss you, man. Sorry we're late."

"Baby." Lucia blows me a kiss but stops to loudly smooch Juniper's cheeks. Junie laughs and squirms away, preferring to play with her cousins than be loved on by Gramma Lucia.

We have been living together now for well over six months and dating for almost ten months, so we decided it's simpler to give everyone family names.

As Juniper learns to talk, I thought it would be a lot easier for her to learn to say Gramma than it would be to say Lucia and then later, if Vito and I get married, start calling her by another name.

As much as I love and adore Vito, and I know

we're both in this for the long haul, we're in no rush to move any faster than this.

He has his own bedroom at our house with blackout curtains so he can sleep when he needs to. His parents have become like the parents I never had and always wanted.

I'm close with Gracie and Chloe, and I've even become close to Ryder since I started working with him at the children's athletics facility he's opened.

"Hey, hey, there she is." Ryder swoops past Ethan and Juniper to kiss me on the cheek. "How'd it go?"

I grin and punch him in the shoulder. "Take a wild guess."

Ryder shrugs. "I don't know."

I clap my hands together and cross my arms over my chest, preening at what I'm about to tell him. "Prepare to be amazed. Seventy kids from the Star Falls community are now enrolled in a fully funded adapted sports league."

"Whoa, whoa. Hold up." Ryder looks at me with his mouth wide open. "I looked at the numbers on Friday. What the heck happened between then and today?"

Vito comes up alongside me and slings an arm over my shoulder. "My girl went out on some calls."

I nod. For the last three months, I've been

working for Ryder's start-up. It turns out that my interest in finance isn't totally going to waste. I have quite the knack for fundraising. He asked me a few months ago if I'd have any interest in seeing what the Star Falls business community's interest would be in sponsoring an adaptive sports league.

Buying specialized equipment like swings and safety gear, not to mention hiring well-trained aides to help run the league, is expensive. Like, made my head swim expensive. But I know there's money out there for good causes, especially for those businesses that want local PR.

You know I went knocking on Michelle's door, and sure enough, she opened the checkbook and donated enough to fund an entire year of sports camps and equipment for one child with special needs.

Ryder had a goal of being able to serve fifty kids, but I wanted to blow that number out of the water.

I spent time while Vito was off on Saturday driving to local businesses and pitching sponsors face-to-face. Turns out, small towns are special places. A bunch of the businesses that hadn't been interested during our phone campaign welcomed me in, listened to my pitch, and opened their checkbooks.

"Holy shit, Eden." Ryder's eyes are wide, and he's

yanking his phone from his pocket. "Does Austin know? I have to tell him."

Lucia comes in from the kitchen, a platter loaded high with homemade meatballs in her arms. "I heard that."

Ryder grimaces and calls out, "Sorry, Ma." Grace slips under his arm and tucks a hand in his back pocket.

"Look at you," Gracie says. "Killing it out there. Keep it up, and Ryder's going to give you an office."

"Marry that woman," Ryder says, pointing at Vito. "Don't let this one go."

"I think he's got me pretty locked down," I say, giving Ryder a grin.

Vito leaves us and heads to the dining room table, where Benito is furiously tapping into his phone. "Yo, idiot," he says, smacking the back of his head. "No phones at the table."

Benito gives his brother the stink eye and smooths his hair back. "You're the idiot. I'm dealing with shit."

"Benito." Mario scowls at Benny over his glasses. "Don't make your mother bring out the swear jar." Pops fills the wineglasses and sets the empty bottle on the table, then grabs a second.

We're a big group now, but Sunday dinner is a

requirement. Chloe and Franco sit knee-to-knee talking, Benny finishes sending his text, while Gracie corrals all her kids to their seats. Vito picks up Junie and places her in his lap—her favorite place to sit during family meals.

"Why are you here anyway?" Gracie needles, lifting a brow at Benito. "You not working today or something?"

Benito strokes his brow with his fingers and waves a hand at his sister. "Is it a crime that I actually want to take a day off? I've got the kitchen covered. I'm going to spend a whole family dinner with my family for once."

Gracie and Vito trade looks, but they leave the issue be. The Bianchis know how to tease one another, but they also know when too much is too much.

There was a time when a family meal like this might have been too much for me. The noise, the heat, the food, the conversation.

But today, I take my seat at the table beside Vito and feel completely at home.

"So," Vito says, clinking a fork against his water glass. "We have a little announcement. It's little, so Ma, get that look off your face. No babies, no weddings. Nothing like that."

Lucia puts a pout on her lips and waves her matching pink nails at her son. "Is it too much for a mother to want more grandchildren? Is that so wrong?"

"Not wrong at all," Mario says, shaking his head. "Go on, son. What's the news?"

"It's not so much news as just an FYI." He leans down to kiss Juniper's cheek. "You guys know Juniper turned two a couple weeks ago."

Ryder pats his belly. "We're still eating leftover cake out of the freezer."

"That's for the kids," Gracie says, shaking her head and giving him a loving squeeze.

"Yeah, well, Juniper got me a little present for her birthday." He moves aside the unbuttoned flannel shirt to reveal a T-shirt that reads: Best Dad in Star Falls.

"Hey," Mario says, followed by a, "That's what I was going to say," from Ryder.

Lucia alone covers her mouth and cries out with joy. "What does this mean, hun? You're not pregnant, you're not getting married…?"

Vito looks at me, and I explain. "Junie's learning so many new words every day. I figured since she's calling all of you by your family names—Gramma and Papa, Auntie and Uncle—we should teach her to…" I stop, my voice catching on the words. My eyes fill with tears, and my nose stings with the happiest kind of joy. "We should teach her to call Vito Dad."

"Oh my God." Lucia jumps up and kisses me and Vito, then lays a loud, juicy smooch on Juniper's cheek.

Mario raises his glass but says, "To one of the best dads in Star Falls."

"The best." Vito corrects.

"I'll fight you on that. I got one of the best dads in town right here," Gracie says.

As the family devolves into a debate over which of the dads in the room is the best, I reach under the table and lace my fingers through Vito's and squeeze.

He's the best man I've ever known. The only father Juniper has ever had.

He's my family, my partner, my friend. Neither one of us really wants to go back to school.

Vito's stopped applying for promotions at work, figuring that any extra time he has, he'd rather spend with our daughter or on our house.

I may not have it all figured out, but I have everything that I really need. Everything I've always wanted.

No matter what the future brings, jobs will come

and go. Money will come and go. But the love I have for these people and this life—that's what's going to stay.

I never dreamed I could have this kind of happiness. And every once in a while, I still get worried that Vito will leave or that Nathan will come back and try to mess up the life I've built for Juniper and myself.

But every time the worries work their way in, I do what I'm doing right now. I reach out and touch the daughter who gives my life meaning. The man who makes me whole.

I have never been happier, and I know Vito and I are going to do everything we can to make this relationship last.

This is what making a life is for me. Imperfect. Loud. Full of people with small-town hearts and open arms.

And as long as I have them, everything else is going to fall into place.

I lift my wineglass and clink it against Vito's, then pass Benito the salad. We eat our meal in the soft glow of the candles on the table, the warmth of the people crammed elbow-to-elbow on more chairs than the table should fit.

We're so close, I can hardly move without bumping into Vito or Benny, but I love it.

As long as I'm part of this extended Bianchi clan, we can never be too close.

Thank you for reading the Star Falls series. I hope you enjoyed reading the Bianchi family as much as I did creating it.